Discord

Leaning Towards Trouble, Volume 2

Lexy Timms

Published by Dark Shadow Publishing, 2019.

DISCORD

First edition. December 3, 2019.

Copyright © 2019 Lexy Timms.

Written by Lexy Timms.

Also by Lexy Timms

We've Been Matched

A "Kind of" Billionaire
Taking a Risk
Safety in Numbers
Pretend You're Mine

BBW Romance Series
Capturing Her Beauty
Pursuing Her Dreams
Tracing Her Curves

Beating the Biker Series
Making Her His
Making the Break
Making of Them

Billionaire Banker Series
Banking on Him
Price of Passion
Investing in Love
Knowing Your Worth
Treasured Forever
Banking on Christmas

Building Billions - Part 1
Building Billions - Part 2
Building Billions - Part 3

Change of Heart Series
The Heart Needs
The Heart Wants
The Heart Knows

Conquering Warrior Series
Ruthless

Counting the Billions
Counting the Days
Counting On You
Counting the Kisses

Diamond in the Rough Anthology
Billionaire Rock
Billionaire Rock - part 2

Dirty Little Taboo Series
Flirting Touch
Denying Pleasure

Dominating PA Series
Her Personal Assistant - Part 1
Her Personal Assistant Box Set

Fake Billionaire Series
Faking It
Temporary CEO
Caught in the Act
Never Tell A Lie
Fake Christmas
Fake Billionaire Box Set #1-3

Firehouse Romance Series
Caught in Flames
Burning With Desire
Craving the Heat
Firehouse Romance Complete Collection

Forging Billions Series
Dirty Money

For His Pleasure
Elizabeth
Georgia

Madison

Fortune Riders MC Series
Billionaire Biker
Billionaire Ransom
Billionaire Misery

Fragile Series
Fragile Touch
Fragile Kiss
Fragile Love

Great Temptation Series
The Devil's Footsteps
Heaven's Command
Mortal's Surrender

Hades' Spawn Motorcycle Club
One You Can't Forget
One That Got Away
One That Came Back
One You Never Leave
One Christmas Night
Hades' Spawn MC Complete Series

Hard Rocked Series
Rhyme
Harmony
Lyrics

Heart of Stone Series
The Protector
The Guardian
The Warrior

Heart of the Battle Series
Celtic Viking
Celtic Rune
Celtic Mann
Heart of the Battle Series Box Set

Heistdom Series
Master Thief
Goldmine
Diamond Heist
Smile For Me
Your Move
Green With Envy

Kissed by Desire
Kissed by Love

Leaning Towards Trouble
Trouble
Discord
Tenacity

Love You Series
Love Life
Need Love
My Love

Managing the Billionaire
Never Enough
Worth the Cost
Secret Admirers
Chasing Affection
Pressing Romance
Timeless Memories

Managing the Bosses Series
The Boss
The Boss Too
Who's the Boss Now
Love the Boss

I Do the Boss
Wife to the Boss
Employed by the Boss
Brother to the Boss
Senior Advisor to the Boss
Forever the Boss
Christmas With the Boss
Billionaire in Control
Billionaire Makes Millions
Billionaire at Work
Precious Little Thing
Priceless Love
Gift for the Boss - Novella 3.5
Managing the Bosses Box Set #1-3

Model Mayhem Series
Shameless
Modesty
Imperfection

Moment in Time
Highlander's Bride
Victorian Bride
Modern Day Bride
A Royal Bride
Forever the Bride

My Best Friend's Sister

Hometown Calling
A Perfect Moment
Thrown in Together

Neverending Dream Series
Neverending Dream - Part 1
Neverending Dream - Part 2
Neverending Dream - Part 3
Neverending Dream - Part 4
Neverending Dream - Part 5

Outside the Octagon
Submit
Fight
Knockout

Protecting Diana Series
Her Bodyguard
Her Defender
Her Champion
Her Protector
Her Forever

Protecting Layla Series
His Mission
His Objective

His Devotion

Racing Hearts Series
Rush

Pace

Fast

Regency Romance Series
The Duchess Scandal - Part 1

The Duchess Scandal - Part 2

Reverse Harem Series
Primals

Archaic

Unitary

RIP Series
Track the Ripper

Hunt the Ripper

Pursue the Ripper

R&S Rich and Single Series
Alex Reid

Parker

Saving Forever
Saving Forever - Part 1
Saving Forever - Part 2
Saving Forever - Part 3
Saving Forever - Part 4
Saving Forever - Part 5
Saving Forever - Part 6
Saving Forever Part 7
Saving Forever - Part 8
Saving Forever Boxset Books #1-3

Shifting Desires Series
Jungle Heat
Jungle Fever
Jungle Blaze

Sin Series
Payment for Sin
Atonement Within
Declaration of Love

Southern Romance Series
Little Love Affair
Siege of the Heart
Freedom Forever
Soldier's Fortune

Whisky Harmony

The Bad Boy Alpha Club
Battle Lines - Part 1
Battle Lines

The Brush Of Love Series
Every Night
Every Day
Every Time
Every Way
Every Touch

The Debt
The Debt: Part 1 - Damn Horse
The Debt: Complete Collection

The Fire Inside Series
Dare Me
Defy Me
Burn Me

The Golden Mail
Hot Off the Press

Extra! Extra!
Read All About It
Stop the Press
Breaking News
This Just In

The Lucky Billionaire Series
Lucky Break
Streak of Luck
Lucky in Love

The Sound of Breaking Hearts Series
Disruption
Destroy
Devoted

The University of Gatica Series
The Recruiting Trip
Faster
Higher
Stronger
Dominate
No Rush
University of Gatica - The Complete Series

T.N.T. Series

Troubled Nate Thomas - Part 1
Troubled Nate Thomas - Part 2
Troubled Nate Thomas - Part 3

Undercover Series
Perfect For Me
Perfect For You
Perfect For Us

Unknown Identity Series
Unknown
Unpublished
Unexposed
Unsure
Unwritten
Unknown Identity Box Set: Books #1-3

Unlucky Series
Unlucky in Love
UnWanted
UnLoved Forever

War Torn Letters Series
My Sweetheart
My Darling
My Beloved

Watch for more at www.lexytimms.com.

DISCORD

LEANING TOWARDS TROUBLE SERIES

USA TODAY BESTSELLING AUTHOR

LEXY TIMMS

Copyright 2019

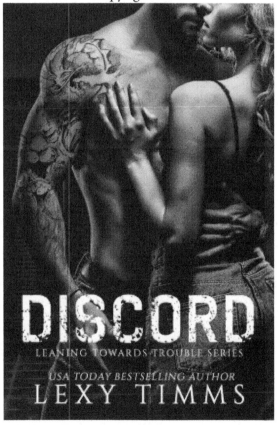

---

1.   http://bookcoverbydesign.co.uk/

Leaning Towards Trouble Series

Book 1 – Trouble
Book 2 – Discord
Book 3 - Tenacity

Find Lexy Timms:

LEXY TIMMS NEWSLETTER:
http://eepurl.com/9i0vD
Lexy Timms Facebook Page:
https://www.facebook.com/SavingForever
Lexy Timms Website:
http://www.lexytimms.com

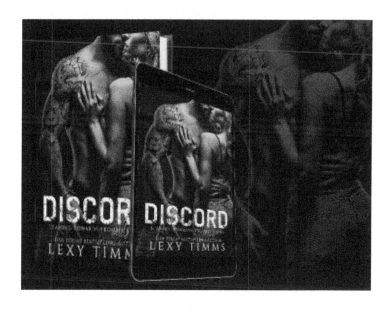

Want to read more...

For **FREE**?

Sign up for Lexy Timms' newsletter

And she'll send you updates on new releases, ARC copies of books

and a whole lotta fun!

Sign up for news and updates!

http://eepurl.com/9i0vD

Discord Blurb

NO MATTER WHAT, TROUBLE always comes round.

The saga continues for Troy and Sadie as they race to beat the clock. He's out there. The dark force that threatens to pull the two of them apart. And the worst part of it is that Troy isn't sure he can keep her safe. She's growing on him. This spindly little girl from his kickboxing classes is getting under his skin. And he knows that spells trouble for the people in his life. He'll become a target. He knows all too well how this kind of thing works. And yet, he can't stay away from her.

Sadie.

The plain-Jane girl who's quickly stealing his heart.

Chapter 1

Sadie

"What are you eating?"

I looked up from my plate and saw a man hovering over me. His suit, tailored specifically to his body. His hands, clasped behind his back. His dark features were alluring, but it was the kind smile on his face that made me smile back.

That made me answer him.

"My favorite combination. Tomato bisque with a ham-and-cheese panini," I said.

He grinned. "I love that adults sometimes never grow out of the good old childhood favorites."

"Every time I got sick, it was tomato soup and cheese sandwiches."

"Not grilled?"

I shook my head. "Nope. The hot cheese burned the roof of my mouth because I'd always be too eager to eat it."

The unfamiliar face smiled even brighter. "I bet you're just as cute now as you were all those years ago as a child."

I set my drink down. "I'm sorry, I don't think I caught your name. I'm Sadie."

And as he sat down in the chair in front of me, he raised his hand. Having his food delivered to my table.

"I'm Luke. It's really nice to meet you, Sadie. Do you mind if I eat with you?"

The moment I first met Luke rushed through my mind. As he shoved the barrel of that gun into my gut, the only thing I focused on was when I first met him. My mind played it over and over. Showcasing all the soft red flags I didn't see in the first place. I wasn't the girl who ever got hit on. Not openly like that. Men always came up to us for Uma. Not me. Not plain-Jane Sadie Marie.

That day, though, Luke found me. Came up to me. Gave me his best face. And because I was too smitten and shell-shocked to see the red flags, he hooked me onto his lure.

Preyed on me, like some wounded animal in the corner.

"You have no idea how much I've missed you. How much I've dreamed about you. How I've longed for you. How many times I've called!"

He yelled the last sentence, and I wondered if anyone would hear. If anyone would hear what was going on and call nine-one-one for me.

When is Troy getting here?

"Why was it so easy for you to leave me?" Luke asked.

There was almost desperation in his voice. But I stood my ground. I girded myself. I didn't want to give him any proof of my fear. Any proof that he had startled me. That was the worst thing I could do. He wanted me scared. He wanted me weak.

He wouldn't get it, though.

Not outwardly, at least.

"Luke," I said softly.

The barrel of the gun wavered against my stomach. I took a small step back, allowing the gun to fall from my body. I gazed up into his stare. His dark eyes, filled with tears and anguish, anger and confusion. Damn, this man really did believe in what he was doing.

And that scared me the most.

"Why did you leave me!?" he roared.

He started waving the gun around in the air and I winced. Fucking hell, I actually winced. And I prayed to heaven on high he didn't accidentally shoot me with that damn thing. It was clear to me he didn't know how to use that weapon. I mean, I didn't either. But I knew what it looked like when someone was proficient with a gun.

And proficient, Luke wasn't.

Troy, please. Where the hell are you?

"Luke, please listen to me," I said.

"Listen to what? You tell me why you left? I'm done arguing with you. You're coming with me." He snarled.

He reached for me, but I took another step back. Which caused him to raise his gun level to my forehead.

"Stop moving away from me!"

I shook my head slowly. "Not until you listen."

He drew in a shuddering breath. "Why can't you just accept my love? That's all I've ever wanted you to do."

"Luke, look at yourself. Look at what you're doing. You haven't hurt me yet. But if you do? Your life changes forever."

"You changed my life forever. I don't want to go back to a life without you."

"Then, you should've treated me with more kindness and compassion instead of always—"

"All I wanted you to do was listen to me." He growled.

"And what you have to understand is that people don't blindly follow one another. I'm a human being, Luke. Not some maid you can boss around," I said.

The gun wavered. "Is that ... what you felt like?"

"What?"

"Did you ... did you feel like my ... my maid?"

I blinked. "Among other things, yes. I did."

He sighed. "I never meant for you to feel that way."

"And that's fine. Just lower the gun, and we can talk, okay?"

"No. You're coming with me. You've always been difficult. You drove me to this."

"If you hurt me, you're going to jail. Simple as that. If you kill me, no one will stop until you've been found."

"I don't want to kill you, Sadie. Come on. I love you. You've always been so damn dramatic."

I shrugged. "From where I'm standing? One pull of that trigger and I *am* dead."

He shook his head. "No. You're going to listen to me."

"That's the problem. You don't—"

"I know what's best for you right now!"

The echoing of his harsh words ricocheted off the corners of my living room.

"A man always knows what's best for the woman he loves. You're mine, Sadie. I made you mine the day I came up to you in that little café and saw you sipping on your tomato soup. Do you remember?"

I swallowed hard. "I could never forget it."

He nodded. "I know. Because it meant a lot to you too. Follow that feeling."

No, because it started my nightmare. "Okay. The feeling. Got it."

"Yes. That feeling. I don't know how the hell you left me the way you did with that feeling trapped inside you. But I forgive you."

I never apologized. "Okay. Thank you."

"Now, as for that man touching you..."

I blinked. "What?"

He straightened his arm out. "Don't you lie to me!"

I held up my hands. "Luke, just calm down. We were doing good at talking. Really, really good. Better than we have in a long time."

He sniffled. "You think?"

I nodded. "I know, Luke. I know how hard it is for you to communicate sometimes. You're doing really well. Don't mess it up now. Okay?"

"It'll uh ... take time for me to forgive you for him. For cheating on me the way you did."

I didn't cheat. "I get it. Okay."

"You're mine, Sadie. Do you hear me?"

But, when I didn't answer him, he charged me.

"You're mine!"

He gripped my arm harder than I'd ever felt him do it before. And had it not been for the gun he shoved against my ribs, I could've taken him down. Turned in to his body and flipped him clear over my fucking shoulder. Slamming him into the ground. But, one pull of that trigger and I was a goner. No hope of ever calling out for nine-one-one, since I didn't know where the hell I put my phone.

"Luke, please," I whispered.

"Get on the couch, you little slut. Now."

He sat me down on the couch. Hard. He pressed his knee into the cushion between my legs as tears rushed my eyes. The gun broke through the first small layer of skin. I whimpered out in pain as his hand grew tighter around my arm. Holy fuck, it hurt. And as much as I wanted to hold back my tears and show no emotion, I couldn't help it.

"You're hurting me," I whispered.

"Just listen. If you'd just *fucking* listen, Sadie."

"No. I won't listen to you anymore. Because listening isn't going to do anything for me but get me more bruises. Right now, you're going to listen to me."

He looked shell-shocked, so I ran with it.

"When I get out of this house, you're going to jail. When the police find you, they're going to lock you away. You've left more than a few red marks this time, Lucas."

"Don't you dare call me that." He growled.

I sneered at him. "I'll call you whatever I want, and if you want to kill me, go ahead. Because I'd rather be dead than risk staring at your face a second longer."

I prepared myself for the inevitable. I prepared myself for my death. There were so many things that flashed through my mind too. Troy. All the things I'd never tell him. Uma. All the places we'd never vacation. My parents. All the things they'd never experience with my life. Like, me getting married. Or me giving them a grandchild. Or Dad, walking me down the aisle.

I made peace with it, though.

I made peace with my death.

"If you want to kill me, go ahead. But you're not getting what you came here for," I said coolly.

Off in the distance, I heard a rumble. It was soft, but I heard it. And my heart leaped to life. Luke snapped his head up as the sound grew closer. And closer. And even closer still.

Then, the sound of sirens followed in stride.

Holy shit, someone heard.

"What did you do?" Luke glowered.

His gaze fell back to mine and I sighed.

"With all that yelling you're doing, did you really think someone wouldn't call?" I asked.

"Fuck!" he exclaimed.

He snatched me up from the couch and tried tugging me toward the back door. The sound of the motorcycle grew closer before it pulled into the driveway. The sirens screamed through the neighborhood. Luke pulled me even closer to the back door of the house. And while I fought him every step of the way, I couldn't wrench from his grasp.

"Let me go!" I shrieked.

"You're coming with me whether you like it or—"

"Let go of her. Now."

Troy's voice sounded like the parting of the heavens. I smelled his cologne as his heavy footsteps sounded through the house. The police sirens grew closer. I looked back and saw Troy leaping over the couch. With his fists balled up, he stared Luke down. His body, positioned to reach out for mine in a heart's beat.

"You." Luke glowered.

"Yes. Me. Get your hands off Sadie, or that ambulance is taking your dead body to a morgue," Troy said.

Luke snickered. "I'd like to see you try that."

Troy took a step toward my ex and I felt Luke flinch. His grip loosened and I tried to pull away, but his hand clamped back down. Tightly. Causing me to whimper yet again.

"He's got a gun," I said softly.

"I know. I see it," Troy said.

Luke grinned. "What, you mean this?"

How the hell were the sirens getting closer, but not actually arriving at the damn house?

"When the police get here, you're going to jail. They'll never let you out. Not with the bruises you've left on me. And not with the prior call record you already have filed away," I said.

"Call record?" Luke asked.

"Yeah. She called after you tugged her into an alleyway on her damn lunch break," Troy said.

Luke blinked. "You called the fucking cops?!"

I nodded. "I did. And I'll keep doing it. If you want your chance to get away, I suggest you run."

"What?" Troy asked.

Luke pulled me closer to his face. "Not unless you're coming with me."

I wanted him caught. But, more than that, I wanted him gone. Away from here. Away from Troy and me. Away from us.

"Run," I whispered.

The sound of wailing sirens mingled together into one glaring sound. And the second lights started flashing through the windows, Luke growled. He shoved me against the wall before ripping my back door open. Slamming it so hard into the wall that the doorknob went through the drywall and paint.

Then he took off across the backyard.

"Sadie," Troy murmured.

Everything felt like a blur. I felt Troy's hands come down against my shoulders, but I pushed him away. I started shaking from head to toe. Tears rushed my eyes and dripped down my cheeks before I could blink them away. I swallowed hard, yet my mouth felt like cotton. I looked around the room as people filtered in. Men in blue uniforms. Paramedics. And though I heard Troy's voice, it felt muffled against my ears.

I felt someone guiding me toward the couch. A soft touch. Possibly a woman? I felt my sleeve being rolled up before blinding flashes of light poured into my vision. I looked over and saw Troy sitting next to me, his eyes filled with worry. And when I looked toward the back door, I saw two men casing my backyard while someone snapped pictures of the doorknob in the wall.

"Why the fuck couldn't you people do something sooner?!"

The tone of Troy's voice ripped me out of my trance. The world came back into clear vision and sounds bustled around me. People talking. Camera shutters closing at rapid speed. The smell of chalk and dust hung heavily in the air for some reason and Troy kept yelling.

Just ... just yelling.

"Look at her. Look at those bruises. He had a damn gun to her, and you couldn't do anything until *now*?"

"Look at it. The gun even left a bruise."

"Look at what's happened to her!"

"Troy, please." I breathed.

I looked over at him as someone softly pulled up my shirt.

"Just stop," I whispered.

It felt like my house was filled with random people for ages. I wanted them all to leave, though. I wanted them gone. I talked them all through what happened as many times as I needed to. In as much detail as they requested. I told them about how he knocked. About how he backed me into my own house with a gun to my stomach. How he tried taking me with him out the back door. About when, exactly, Troy made his way into the house. They took notes and listened carefully. Like they should've done before. And after all was said and done, the police officers closed my back door. Made their way out of my house. Drove their cars and ambulances and fire trucks into the night, leaving me there to stew in my own fear.

I made sure the doors were locked, though. Windows too.

"Do you want to stay here for the night?" Troy asked.

The hole in the wall sat there. Gaping at me. Reminding me of the events of the night. Troy stood next to me by the couch, his eyes gazing at my profile. I needed sleep. And I knew I wouldn't get it in this house tonight.

I slowly shook my head. "No. I don't want to stay here."

"You could come stay at my place, if you want."

I sighed. "I really don't care. Just not here."

So, he took my hand. Guiding me toward my front door as I picked up the suitcases I had packed for my next Florida journey for work.

"Come on. We'll go stay at my place for the night and figure out what to do in the morning," he said.

But something told me I'd have to postpone this Florida trip too.

And for some reason, that really bothered me.

Chapter 2

Troy

S he clung to me with dear life as she rode on the back of my bike. And while it should have felt marvelous, tonight it only filled me with anger. Those bruises. The ones on her arm and her ribs. They made me angrier than I'd ever been in my entire life. The fury rushing through my veins shook my core. Made the marrow of my bones vibrate. My vision dripped with red, making it hard to see as I navigated us back to my condo.

But I got us there safely.

"Come on, let's get you upstairs," I said softly.

I scooped Sadie into my arms, and she curled against my chest. I left the to-go tray of food in the storage compartment of my bike, ready to be cleaned out in the morning. I wanted to make her something fresh. She needed something soft on her stomach too. Soup or a light salad. Or possibly a small pasta dish with a bit of sauce.

I'd make her whatever she wanted, so long as she was in my care.

I walked us into my condo complex and started right for the elevator. I felt people staring at us, but I didn't care. Because all that mattered was making sure Sadie was safe. She was silent, until we got into my condo. Until I settled her on the couch. Because when I did, she reached for my hand.

Tugging at me to sit next to her.

"You hungry?" I asked.

She shook her head as I sat down beside her.

"Just sit with me," she said softly.

Her head leaned against my shoulder and I closed my eyes. Her hand slid down my arm, until her fingers intertwined with mine. I did as she asked. Though, I wanted to feed her. I wanted something to do. I needed something to pour this angry energy into.

I need to call Wren.

I stuffed my free hand into my pocket and dug around for my phone. And when I pulled it out, I decided against a phone call. I wasn't sure how Sadie would feel with me talking out loud about what just happened. So, I opened up a text message to Wren. And Paris. And Uma ... since I had her information stored away for the kickboxing and self-defense classes.

Me: Luke came after her again tonight. The police got involved. Sadie's at my place for the night. Uma, I locked up the house. But there's a hole in the wall near the back door. I'll explain more later. Just wanted to let you guys know.

I sent the message off and Sadie moved away from me. I looked over at her and watched her settle her head against a pillow on the other side of the couch. I wanted to pull her back. But she'd been through a lot tonight already. And if she didn't want to be touched, that was her right.

"You want a blanket?" I asked.

But all she did was shrug.

I pulled a blanket from the back of the couch and covered us both up with it. I watched her curl up, putting distance between us.

"Are you upset with me?" I asked.

"Why would I be?" Sadie asked softly.

"I ... don't know."

"No. I'm not."

The air was still tense, though. And I wanted more than anything to alleviate it.

We sat there in silence as Sadie's eyes opened and closed. Opened, and closed. Like she was trying to sleep, then couldn't. Trying to sleep, then couldn't. I hated not being able to touch her. Though, I understood it. I hated not being able to comfort her. Though, I understood that too. I'd been inconsolable after Holly. After everything that went down with my own ex. I understood—at least, somewhat—the headspace Sadie was in right now.

So, as much as I wanted to go against it, I followed her lead.

"Troy?"

Wren's voice filtered through the door before a soft knock fell against it. I whipped my head around before looking back over at Sadie. But she didn't move.

"Hey, open the door. It's locked," Paris said.

"Let them in," Sadie whispered.

So, I got up from the couch.

The smell of food followed Wren inside before Paris came in after him. He had bags of food while Paris had ice cream by the ton. And before I got the door closed, I felt something fighting my ability to do so.

"Hey there. Seems like I'm right on time," Uma said.

"Uma?" Sadie asked.

I ushered her in. "Come on. Yeah."

"The hospital let me leave work early. Where is she?" Uma asked.

"The couch," I murmured.

"All right. I've got some fresh groceries for things to cook later along with hot soup, fresh bread, premade salads, some piping-hot macaroni-and-cheese, and all sorts of things to drink. Oh and beer," Wren said. "You always need beer during times like these."

"And I've got different kinds of ice cream. Everything from red velvet to orange sherbet to mint chocolate chip. They had half pints, so I took it as an excuse to get every flavor," Paris said.

I grinned. "Of course you did."

"Hey there, beautiful. How ya feeling?" Uma asked.

And when Paris walked over to the couch, I figured the girls needed time to talk through things anyway. So, I made my way into the kitchen, where Wren was putting shit up.

"I really appreciate all this," I said.

"The hell else did you expect us to do? Sit by after getting a text like that?" he asked.

I shrugged. "I don't really know right now, to be honest."

"The fuck happened tonight?" he whispered.

I shoved the nineteen different flavors of ice cream in my freezer before I sighed.

"From what I can tell, Luke figured out where she lived and came over. With a gun," I murmured.

"He had a what now?" Wren asked.

I peeked into the living room and saw the girls gathered on the couch. Paris and Uma had Sadie upright and talking. Which was a good sign. And it made me feel a little better in terms of telling Wren what happened.

"Yeah, he had a gun," I said softly.

"Tell me you killed him."

I snickered. "I want to. I really do."

"At least tell me the cops were called."

I nodded. "I was traveling into the neighborhood when I heard the sirens kick up. And when they did? I just knew, you know? In the pit of my gut, I knew what was happening. So, I got to the house as quickly as I could. Even though there wasn't a car or anything in the driveway, the front door was wide fucking open."

"Shit," he whispered.

"And when I got there, he had her in his grip. Hard. Had a gun pointed at her. I'd never seen her so calm, though."

"I'm sorry, calm?"

I nodded. "Yeah. Calm and collected. The second I saw that rat bastard's face, I envisioned seven different ways of killing him with my bare hands. Yet, Sadie kept talking to him in a soft, even tone. She kept her cool under pressure, and I've got no clue how she did it."

He put his hand on my shoulder. "How are *you* feeling, dude?"

I chuckled bitterly. "I want to find that asshole and kill him."

"So, I take it he bolted before the cops really got there."

"More than that. She told him to run, Wren."

"What?"

"Yeah. She told him to get out of there. I don't know why either. I'm still trying to figure that one out."

He blinked. "You think she's trying to save him?"

I shook my head. "I don't think so. I mean, I don't really know, but I don't think that's it."

"You think she just wanted him gone? Didn't want to deal with all the fuss of him being arrested and all that?"

I looked back over at the girls and saw Sadie crying against Uma's shoulder.

"I really don't know, Wren."

He squeezed my shoulder. "It's going to be okay. Now, the police can do all they can to keep her safe."

"I hope you see to that."

"Trust me, I couldn't do much after that incident that happened in the alleyway. But I can now."

I sighed. "I listened to her tell the cops what happened, man. She was—so strong. So strong during the entire thing. I mean, he had her. In his grasp. With a gun at her side, Wren. But, I wanted to kill that man."

"I know you did."

My stare found his. "No, you don't get it, Wren."

"Troy, take a breath."

"I *want* to kill him. As in, it's all I can think about."

He took both of my shoulders and stared at me. Hard.

"You need to ground yourself, Troy. I know you're angry right now. But, you can't turn into him in order to beat him. He came prepared to kill Sadie tonight. He came with a gun. He came to do harm. You can't turn into him to beat him. She'll never forgive you for it."

I sighed. "I need a fucking beer."

He snickered. "Good thing Paris bought a twenty-four pack."

He released me and opened the fridge before grabbing each of us a drink. I cracked it open and chugged it down, not stopping until the damn thing was gone. Then, Paris poked her head into the kitchen and started gathering up some food.

"She's hungry," she said.

"Good. She needs to eat," I said.

"You guys can come join us whenever you want," Uma said.

"I don't want to crowd her," Wren said.

"Me neither," I said.

"You're not crowding her. She just ... needed a second to process. I think she's gotten the worst of it out of her system. So, come on over whenever you guys want to," Paris said.

"After another beer, yeah," I said.

Wren and I shared another drink while the girls ate on the couch. And when we walked back over, we found that the girls had eaten all the soup. Most of the pasta too.

"Looks like ice cream's in order," Wren said.

"Did someone say something about mint chocolate chip?" Sadie asked.

I nodded. "Yeah. Want me to get you some?"

"I want that red velvet," Uma said.

"And I'll take the Cherry Garcia," Paris said.

Sadie's eyes ventured up toward mine and my heart broke for her. They were red. Bloodshot. Swollen, from all the crying she had done. But, through it all, a soft smile crossed her face.

"Thank you," she said softly.

"You don't ever have to thank me, Sadie. Okay?" I said.

"Ice cream. Troy. Go. Now," Paris commanded.

"Please?" Sadie asked.

I smiled. "Anything for you."

I walked back into the kitchen and gathered the supplies. All the spoons and ice cream our hearts desired. By the time I got back to the couch, Sadie was actually giggling with the girls. Giggling! While Wren cracked jokes and told insane stories of his week at work. And while her soft laughter quelled the quiet rage within my heart, it didn't stop my bloodlust.

I still wanted to wring Luke's neck.

Or chop his hands off so he can't ever touch Sadie again.

"So, hate to break it to you, Troy. But, we aren't leaving Sadie tonight," Paris said.

"Yeah, we can't leave our girl in this kind of condition," Uma said.

"You guys, I'm going to be fine," Sadie said.

"If Sadie wants you guys here, then you're more than welcome to stay," I said.

Sadie looked over at me. "Really?"

I nodded. "Of course. Do you want them to stay?"

She looked up at me sheepishly before nodding.

"That would be nice," she said.

I grinned. "Then you guys are staying. Hate to break it to you."

Uma giggled. "I know, such a punishment after getting off work early."

Paris laughed. "Looks like you and Wren are sleeping together, though."

Uma nodded. "Yep. Apparently, you've got a massive king-size bed in your room."

"Which can easily sleep the three of us," Sadie said.

"I should've known we'd be kicked out like that," Wren said.

I chuckled. "If that's how you guys wanna do the sleeping arrangements tonight, then I have no issues cuddling with Wren."

"Just don't get mad when I cop a feel," he said.

I rolled my eyes. "I'd be offended if you didn't, asshole."

"You sexy thing," Wren said playfully.

"Oh boy," Sadie said.

"We've started something," Paris said.

"Looks like you two might lose your boyfriends to this shit right here," Uma said.

Sadie's eyes found mine and I could've sworn I saw a twinkle in her eye. I mean, we hadn't talked about what we were officially yet. But, she didn't correct Uma in her statement. A good start I supposed, considering what went on tonight. And while part of me wanted to be with Sadie in my bed for the evening, I understood the arrangements.

Even if I did want to fight the girls on it.

Chapter 3

Sadie

I woke up with arms and legs tossed over my body and I felt ... well, I felt disoriented. I stared up at a ceiling I didn't recognize, and it took me a few seconds to get my bearings. I blinked the sleep away as bodies shifted next to me. I drew in deep breaths as I tried to figure out where the hell I was and who the fuck was beside me.

But once it all came crashing back? I shivered.

Which woke Uma up.

"Sadie?" she murmured.

I heard Paris groan as she rolled over before falling back to sleep.

"Uma?" I whispered.

"I'm right here. Hey, girl," she said.

I lobbed my head over and saw my best friend staring back at me.

"You okay?" she asked.

My eyes watered. "No."

"Does your arm still hurt?"

"Yeah."

"What about your ribs?"

"Mm-hmm."

"Want me to get you some Tylenol of some sort?"

I shook my head. "Please, don't leave."

She wiped at my tears. "Okay, okay. Don't panic. I'm not going anywhere."

I sniffled. "Why is this shit happening to me?"

She shook her head softly. "I don't know, Sadie. I wish I had an answer for you. But, I don't."

"Why is he such a dickweed?"

"Again, I don't know."

"I wish someone did."

"I know you do."

Paris groaned. "It's because he's a small-dicked asshole who got fucked in the brain by someone, so now he figures he can take it out on other people around him."

I stared at Uma with wide eyes before the two of us started giggling.

"Did you just say 'small-dicked'?" I asked.

Paris rolled over. "Yeah. I mean, he probably is."

Uma giggled. "I remember some of the stories. He definitely is."

I blushed. "You're so mean."

Paris nudged me playfully. "See? Small-dicked and insecure. They always are."

I sighed as I stared up at the ceiling. Then, I inhaled deeply. Drawing in the most amazing scent imaginable.

"What is that?" I asked.

Uma sniffed the air. "That's definitely coffee."

Paris sniffed it too. "And ... bagels?"

I looked between the two girls before we slid out of bed. We shuffled our way out of the bedroom, finding Troy already in the kitchen. There was a full pot of coffee already on the coffee table in his living room. There were toasted bagels slathered in peanut butter as well as cream cheese. And in the middle, a small bowl of fruit.

"Eat up, you guys. Because once Wren wakes up, the rest of it will be gone," Troy said.

"I heard that," Wren murmured.

We all sat down on the couch and ate. Well, all of us except Uma. I wasn't sure where she had gotten off to. But my stomach didn't care either. Troy poured me a massive mug of coffee with the best sweet cream around. And after filling my stomach with two entire bagels full to the brim with cream cheese, Uma finally emerged.

"So, I just got off the phone with the police," she said.

My entire body tensed up as my eyes whipped over to her.

"What did they say?" Paris asked.

"What's going on?" Wren asked.

I felt Troy's hand fall against my shoulder. Trying to comfort me with a soft squeeze.

"I mean, it's not necessarily bad," Uma said.

"What's going on?" I asked.

She sighed. "So, the police are back at the house trying to find more evidence. There are men casing the backyard and the woods to try and find out where Luke ran off to. They're also going to have someone come in and spackle that hole up in the wall. Though, we'll have to go out and find paint to match it so we can paint over it."

I nodded slowly. "What else?"

"Until the house is cleared, we can't go back. They want to try and find as much evidence of his presence as they can. You know, other than eyewitness testimony."

I sighed. "He didn't touch anything but me."

"Well, maybe he dropped some hair on the ground or something. And he did rip the back door open. Maybe there's some fingerprints."

"Yeah. Maybe," I said flatly.

"They'll get him, Sadie. I know they will," Troy said.

And while I knew he was trying to be comforting, it didn't do much to comfort me.

Why had I told him to run again?

Oh, right. Because you're an idiot.

"Well, at least I grabbed the clothes I packed up for Florida," I said.

"You aren't seriously thinking about taking that trip this week, are you?" Uma asked.

I shrugged. "Why not? Work's all I've got right now as a distraction. Why wouldn't I take it?"

"She's right. Work can be a great antidote during things like this," Wren said.

"And she can keep coming to classes too," Paris said.

"Shit. Workout clothes," I murmured.

"Don't worry. We can go out and buy you a cheapo pair for now. Those classes will really help to distract you," Paris said.

"Do you want to try and go into work today?" Troy asked.

"I still think she should take today and rest. Just rest," Uma said.

I sighed. "Noted, and thank you. But I really need to get to work. I need something to do other than sit around here and stew in what happened last night."

"Attagirl," Wren said.

I knew Uma still wasn't happy with my decision. But she'd have to be. I stood up and hugged everyone before they made their exits, leaving me and Troy with a massive breakfast that still needed to be eaten. Troy walked everyone out, giving me a few seconds alone. To myself. To breathe, and think, and reflect.

Before he came back inside and closed the door behind him.

"What can I do for you right now?" he asked.

I smiled softly. "You're a good man, you know that?"

"I just want you safe. And happy. That's all."

I turned around. "That's what makes you so good, Troy."

"It's the least you deserve from someone."

"There is something you can do for me, though."

He took a step toward me. "You name it."

"Take me to work?"

He smiled. "My pleasure."

I took the liberty of a long, hot shower. Washing away the sins and fears of last night to try and put myself in a decent frame of mind for the beginning of my week. Monday was upon us, and I had articles to write. Things to plan. Articles to get to my editor and plans to make. I scrubbed myself down not once, but twice. And as much as I tried to leave them be, I let my fingers drift along my bruises. Along the sharp circle against my ribs, reminding me of the barrel of that gun as it pressed into my flesh. Along Luke's handprint as it etched itself into my skin. The bruise growing darker and darker. Seemingly, before my very eyes.

Why didn't I listen to the red flags earlier?

I got ready for work and Troy escorted me into the office. I clung to him, soaking in his warmth and his strength, and trying to fill my own tank. He parked his bike on the curb and I slid off. I was getting used to riding it. And I found that I enjoyed it. He smiled at me before leaning in, kissing me softly against my cheek. I felt myself blushing at the touch. But, instead of pulling away like I figured I would have, I leaned a bit deeper into his lips.

Feeling them linger against my skin.

"Call me if you need anything. Absolutely anything. Okay?" Troy asked.

I nodded. "Maybe we could grab lunch."

He grinned. "I'd love that. You let me know what time, and I'll be here."

"Around twelve thirty? I'll have an hour."

"I'll be here right at twelve thirty, then."

I smiled. "Perfect."

He revved his engine before pulling away from the curb. And as I watched him merge back into traffic, I felt my safety net buckling. Troy was my safety net. The one person I could count on to always try and protect me. And the farther away he rode, the more vulnerable I felt. But the feeling didn't last for long. Especially once I heard my editor's voice behind me.

"What happened, Sadie?"

I whipped around and saw his eyes against my arm. And when I looked down, I saw the bruise peeking out from the sleeves of my shirt.

I tugged at the fabric until the bruise was covered up again. But the damage had already been done.

"Can we talk in your office?" I asked.

He nodded. "Of course. Come on."

He led me into his office and promptly shut the door behind me. He made his way to his desk, but didn't sit. Instead, he stood. With worry filling his eyes, his hands slid into his pockets. Waiting for me to start.

"How much do you already know?" I asked.

He shrugged. "The police might have called to inform me of what happened."

"Is that protocol for something like this?"

"I'm not sure. I've never been in this scenario before."

I snickered. "Me neither."

He nodded slowly. "I'm going to postpone the Florida trip."

"No, no, no. Please. Please, don't do that."

"I'm not sending you—"

"I need work. I need work to distract me."

"And I'm not telling you that you can't work. I'm just telling you that you're in no condition to travel. It's not a big deal, Sadie. I'm just going to reschedule it for a couple of weeks out. Just until you can..."

His eyes fell back to my arm and I got what he was trying to say.

"Until I can heal," I said softly.

He shrugged. "It's nothing against you. I just have to try and juggle—"

I held up my hand. "I'm not upset with you. I just don't want you to put me on leave because you think I need it. Work is all I have right now. Don't take that from me."

He grinned. "From the state of that kiss this morning, I doubt it's the *only* thing you have."

I blushed. "You saw that?"

He came out from around his desk. "Sadie, I think it's fantastic that you've found someone else. Especially in this insane situation you're in. I have to reschedule the Florida trip. But, in the meantime, it's local business as usual. I've already emailed you this morning about the two places I want you to write reviews on. One's a nice restaurant, and the other one is a spa."

I narrowed my eyes. "You did that on purpose, didn't you?"

"I don't know what you're talking about. It's a new spa that's opened up in town, and my wife claims to love it. Figured you could give it a try and write up a nice review."

"Uh-huh."

"You said you wanted to work, right?"

I smiled. "Yes, I do."

"Then, get to your desk and get working. Daylight's already burning, Sadie."

He ushered me out of his office and I happily walked over to my desk. But, the shaking of my hands didn't stop. It grew hard to type. Hard to edit. Hard to concentrate. I constantly looked over my shoulder to see if anyone was watching me. Or to see if Luke had come into my place of work to track me down again.

Yeah. You need some spa time.

Despite constantly keeping my eye on the clock, lunchtime rolled around quickly. And while I knew Troy was meeting me right at twelve thirty, it didn't stop me from being afraid to leave my office. What if Luke was out there? Watching? Waiting for me, or something?

"Sadie?"

I swiveled my chair around at the sound of his voice.

"Hey, Troy."

"You okay? It's a quarter to one," he said.

I blinked. "I'm sorry. I must've gotten caught up in work."

He thumbed over his shoulder. "There's a Korean barbecue food truck up the road. Want to go get some?"

"Actually, could you bring me something back? We could eat at my desk."

His eyes danced between mine. "You sure?"

I nodded. "Yep. I'm sure."

"Okay. I can do that. You want anything specific?"

"Surprise me."

His eyes narrowed softly, but he did as I asked. And when I watched him walk out the double doors of my building's headquarters, I let out the breath I had been holding. I turned myself back around and stared at my phone. Listening as it taunted me. As it urged me to do the one thing I needed to do from the beginning.

So, I picked up the phone and dialed Mom's number.

"Sweetie? Isn't it the middle of your workday?"

I forced a smile. "Hey, Mom."

"Hon! Sadie's on the phone!" Mom exclaimed.

I heard the click of the speakerphone button before Dad's voice sounded in my ear.

"Everything okay, princess? You good?" he asked.

I sighed. "Actually, uh…"

"Honey? What's wrong?" Mom asked.

"What do you need?" Dad asked.

Tears rushed my eyes as I leaned back in my chair.

"There's something I have to tell you guys," I said.

"What is it? You can tell us anything," Mom said.

"Something wrong with the house? Did you break a window or something?" Dad asked.

I snickered. "Not exactly. Though, there is a hole in the wall."

"Oh, honey. That's an easy fix," Mom said.

"Is that why you called us?" Dad asked.

"No," I whispered.

"You're worrying me. Talk to us," Mom said.

I sniffled. "Luke and I aren't together anymore."

"Oh, princess," Dad said.

"I'm so sorry, honey. What happened?" Mom asked.

I pinched the bridge of my nose. "He started getting angry all the time. Yelling. We fought more than we should have."

The phone call stayed silent as I tried gathering my thoughts.

"He, uh..."

"Did he put his hands on you?" Dad growled.

"Calm down," Mom whispered.

"Actually, he did," I said.

"What?" Mom asked flatly.

"That's it. I knew that boy was trouble. We're coming up there. We're packing our bags now," Dad said.

"No, no, no, no. Just ... just listen. The police are involved and—"

"The *police*?" Mom exclaimed.

"Why are the police involved? What happened? Tell us everything, Sadie," Dad said.

I did as they asked. I told them everything. And the more I spoke, the angrier my father became. Mom started crying. Dad started cursing. And as I dove into what happened last night, I practically heard the zippers on his luggage closing shut.

"We're headed your way. We'll be there by tomorrow morning," Dad said.

"I've got Troy here," I said quickly.

Everything fell silent before Mom piped up.

"Who's Troy?" she asked.

I swallowed hard. "Just—a guy here who's helping me. He and a bunch of friends I've made from the kickboxing classes helped me out last night. I stayed at his place. I mean, we all did."

"This Troy someone I should know?" Dad glowered.

"Not yet, I don't think," I said.

"Not yet?" Mom asked.

I sighed. "Look, I love you guys. So much. But, Troy is helping me with things back here. Along with Uma, and Paris. And Wren. New friends, and all that. I promise, I'm okay," I said.

"You're not okay. And that's all right," Mom said.

"I'm coming to see you." Dad hissed.

"Just do this for me, okay? Please, there's nowhere for you to stay anyway. The house is an active crime scene right now. And until then, Uma's staying with a nurse friend of hers and I'm staying with Troy," I said.

"We really need to meet this guy," Mom said.

"Please, don't come. I'll see you guys in a couple of weeks when I come down for work," I said.

"I thought you were coming down this week?" Dad asked.

I sighed. "My editor felt it best to postpone the trip until I could screw my head back on straight."

The phone call fell silent again before an arm came into view. An arm attached to food that smelled divine.

"You call us every day," Dad said.

"Yes, every day with updates," Mom said.

I nodded. "I can do that."

I looked up and saw Troy wink at me. Making my cheeks heat.

"And you call us again tonight. So we can talk more," Dad said.

"I don't like this one bit," Mom murmured.

Troy pulled up a chair as I reached for my drink.

"Thank you, guys. I love you," I said.

"We love you too," Mom said.

And after we said our goodbyes, I hung up the phone.

Ready to eat my lunch with the only person who made me feel safe anymore.

Chapter 4

Troy

I walked into my guest bedroom and saw Uma curled up against Sadie. For the second time that week, Sadie woke up with fits of nightmares that caused her to call her best friend. And while I couldn't blame her for it, part of me wanted to be the one to comfort Sadie. To be the one curled up next to her and soothing those fears and horrors away.

Sadie had been at my place for the past few nights. The workweek was winding down, and her house would be available for her today. I had mixed feelings about that shit. I mean, on the one hand? I wanted her to feel safe in her own home again. The police had followed through on hiring someone to fix that hole in the wall. I even took the girls paint shopping yesterday to find a paint that matched. You know, so they could paint over it. But, part of me wanted to try and convince Sadie to finish the week here.

I wanted to be able to touch her, and see her. Make sure, with my own two eyes, that she was safe.

I didn't want her forty minutes away in a completely different city.

It sucked. But I wasn't about to take away her agency. Not after all she had been through. So, I sucked it up and played the "happy lover" card. Whenever she talked about finally being back at her place, I nodded and grinned. Whenever she talked about finally sleeping in her own bed once more, I plastered on my best smile. I'd miss fixing her dinner every night. Coming home from the gym to see her on the couch. Doing research for another article. I'd miss her riding on the back of my bike while cruising around the city. Or walking back with me from the gym.

I'd miss having her around all the time like that.

Still, this was her decision. And if she wanted to go back home, then that was a testament to her mental strength. Not many people could long for a place like that. A place where they had been assaulted. A place that had been invaded by something as terrible as an abusive ex. In some ways, I was in awe of her strength. How far she had come. How stable she had forced herself to be.

But it didn't change how much I wanted to tell her to stay put.

To stay with me.

I found myself cutting my days shorter, though. Going home right at five thirty instead of staying late. Instead of closing down the gym. I found myself running a more regular schedule just to get home to her. Just to spend more time with her. I even took a more regular lunch to make sure I had that time with her too. Having Sadie in my life and in my condo changed the way I ran things. The way I operated. And for the better too.

I wondered if I'd be able to keep it up after she went home.

I made my way into the kitchen and put on a pot of coffee. I scrambled up some eggs and fried some bacon, letting the smell drift over to the bedroom. I enjoyed cooking for Sadie. Watching her eat my creations and hum over how good they were. Yet another thing I'd miss about this dynamic we had together.

And when I heard the girls stirring in bed, I started making them plates.

"Something smells good in here," Uma murmured.

"Mmm, coffee." Sadie hummed.

I poured two mugs and walked them over to the girls as they flopped down on the couch. I handed off the mugs before gathering the plates and silverware to bring over. I wanted to eat with them, but I couldn't. I needed to start pulling away from Sadie now in order to make the transition easier. On my part, at least. Sure, that sounds self-ish. But I had to protect myself a little bit.

Because letting Sadie go back to that house without me there to protect her gave me enough anxiety to deal with on my own.

"You not going to eat with us?"

Sadie's voice turned me around just before I got to my bedroom door.

"I ate while I was cooking up things. Plus, I need to be in the office soon," I said.

"Oh, okay. Well, have a good day," she said.

And when she gave me that sleepy little smile of hers, my heart skipped a beat.

"I definitely will. Oh, and wear something warm. It's supposed to be storming all day," I said.

Sadie pointed at me. "Noted."

I walked back into my bedroom just as my cell phone started ringing. I rushed over to it and swiped it off my bedside table, then slipped into the bathroom. I closed the door before I picked it up, knowing damn good and well who was calling.

It was who called me every morning around this time.

With an update on the search for Luke.

"Tell me you've got something," I said.

Wren sighed. "We had a possible spotting of him on the other side of town. But, it was a false alarm."

"Damn it," I murmured.

"It's like he's vanished without a trace. It doesn't make any sense. It's not like he's got the means to do it either."

"What do you mean?"

"What I mean is, the man isn't overly wealthy. He doesn't have a passport. Hell, the last car he had registered in his name he totaled three years ago, and hasn't bought one since. I don't know how a man like him, without those resources, can still fall off the damn radar."

"And you've had his place staked out?"

"Yep. For the past four days."

I sighed. "And he hasn't come back once?"

Wren snickered. "Trust me, if he had? He'd be in custody right now."

"What about friends? Family in the area?"

"We've already ticked off those boxes. I promise you, we're doing what we can."

I growled. "Well, it's not good enough."

"Hey, this is me you're talking to."

I sighed heavily. "I'm sorry. I'm sorry. It's just—"

"I know you're worried for her. We all are. Me, included. This is personal. For a lot of us. Especially once the evidence came back."

I paused. "What evidence?"

"Well, apparently Luke has a couple of friends in my precinct. They were really bucking against all this shit going on. Claiming he couldn't do something like this."

"Of course, they would."

"But, fingerprints were found on the doorknob. They came back as a match for Luke."

"Wait, that means he has a record."

He snickered. "Yeah, and it's not a good one. He's had several unproven phone calls directed toward him that range from assault and battery to domestic arguments that disturbed neighbors. This shit is right up his alley. And once the hair fibers came—"

"Hair fibers? How much have you been holding out on me?"

"Will you let me do my damn job, Troy?"

"You told me you'd keep me updated."

"And I am. But, as an officer, I also have protocol that has to be followed. Okay?"

I paused. "Yeah. Yeah. Okay. So, hair fibers. From the house?"

"Yeah. The floors. It's undoubted proof that he was there. It's turned the couple of friends he has in this precinct around. So, now we're all doing what we can to find him. And we will find him. It's just going to take us time."

I sighed. "Are you sure that house is safe for her to go back to? Because now that it's been released, she'd dead set on going back there."

"Not only is it safe, but that area is going to be patrolled more heavily. I've already put in the request to work with their police precinct and gotten it approved. We're all working together on this now. And as much as a patrol car can get out there, they'll be out there."

"No one can stake out her house or something? You know, sit out there for protection?"

"We don't have those kinds of resources right now. Her case isn't the only case we're all working on. But, once resources can be freed up, that's exactly what I plan on doing with them."

I pinched the bridge of my nose. "All right. Thanks for the phone call."

"Anytime. I gotta get back to work. I'll call tomorrow morning."

"Thanks. I appreciate it."

"Yep."

I hung up the phone and dragged myself into the shower. I washed myself down and got ready for my day in the office. And when I emerged in my work clothes, I found Sadie still sitting on the couch. Wrapped up in a blanket. With a mug of coffee in her hands and her laptop on her thighs.

"Everything okay?" I asked.

She nodded mindlessly, but didn't say anything.

"Whatcha watching?" I asked.

"The news," she said.

I walked behind her and peered over her shoulder. She sipped her coffee as the shower in my guest bedroom struck up. And I figured Uma was getting ready for her own workday. Sadie's eyes were glued to her laptop screen. I knew why too. She was looking for anything that might prove to her Luke had been caught. That he'd been taken down and dragged away for the whole world to witness.

"You can work from here if you want to," I said.

Sadie nodded slowly. "Thanks. I might do that."

I bent down and kissed the top of her head.

"Want me to work from here too?" I murmured.

She shook her head. "No, I'm okay."

"You sure?"

"Yeah."

I kissed her head again. "All right. Well, call me if you need anything. Okay?"

She tilted her head back. "I will. I promise."

My eyes found hers and I wanted nothing more than to kiss her lips. But I didn't want to push her. I wanted her to know I still held affection for her. But I didn't want to rush into territory she wasn't ready for. The look in her eyes was loving. However, there was hesitation as well. Enough to make me resist the urge to drop my mouth against hers.

"Well, have a good day," I said.

She blinked. "You too. Okay?"

I kissed her forehead. "I promise."

As much as I hated it, I forced myself toward the door. I forced myself to go to work. I forced myself to go to my office at the gym. I really needed a different office for my accounting shit. Maybe later, though. Once I helped dig the damn gym out of the renovation debt we still had. I made my way to the parking garage underneath the complex and slipped into my car. It was already pouring down rain, and I sure as hell wasn't about to walk to work in shitty weather. I hated how long it took me to drive up the road, though. A five-minute walk versus an almost fifteen-minute drive. It was fucking insane, if I had to say anything about it.

Still, nothing beat getting into work completely dry while everyone else looked like a drowned rat.

"Morning, Troy."

I nodded. "Morning, Paris."

I heard her drop some papers before she quickly took up space at my side.

"So, how is she?"

I sighed. "Sadie?"

"Well, duh. How's she doing? I want to text her, like, all the time. But I figured that's a little too much."

I grinned. "Maybe."

"Are you going to answer my question?"

"Once we get into my office."

I unlocked my space and let her in. Then, I slipped in and closed the door behind me.

"Is it bad? It's got to be bad," Paris said.

"She's doing as well as she can right now. But, I'm pretty sure she's set on going back to the house today," I said.

"What? So soon? Is she ready for something like that?"

"I don't know. But, when the police called her and told her the house had been released back to her, it was the first time in days I've genuinely seen her smile."

"Wow."

"Yeah. She's missing home. It just makes me anxious to know she's going back."

"Trust me, it makes all of us anxious."

I ran my hand down my face. "Good to know."

Paris clapped my upper arm with her hand. "How *you* holding up?"

I snickered. "I'm not. But, I'm trying my best."

"Could've fooled me."

"Thanks?"

"You're welcome?"

I grinned. "Thank you for all you and Wren have done for Sadie this week."

She waved her hand in the air. "Ah, it's not a problem. Oh, Wren's still contacting you in the mornings, right?"

"He is, yeah. We talked about an hour ago."

"Good. Okay. I want to make sure he keeps up with those."

I smiled. "Already getting on his case, huh?"

She shrugged. "He promised, and I just want to make sure he keeps good on his promise."

"Wren always keeps good on his word. I've never once had to question that."

"I know, I know. I guess it's just my way of helping behind the scenes."

"And I appreciate that. Really."

We stared at each other for a few seconds.

"Well, I should get back to the front desk."

I nodded. "And I have some numbers to crunch."

"Is work helping you?"

I snickered. "I guess I should say yes."

"Okay. Well, you're not alone in that. So, don't feel out of place for it."

"Thank you for that, actually."

She giggled. "Glad my unproductivity can help."

She saw herself out of my office and I looked down at my desk. The numbers hadn't helped me all week. And I knew they wouldn't help me today. Still, I sat down and got to work. Filling out paperwork, entering in new members to the gym, and responding to emails from my outside accounting clients.

All the while, trying to resist the urge to cancel the kickboxing class for tonight.

Chapter 5

Sadie

Troy: I haven't canceled kickboxing class tonight. You should try to come. Might help you blow off some steam. And if you want, I can give you some more self-defense teaching after class.

I read Troy's message over and over. On the one hand, I wanted to go to class. And on the other hand, I had something more important I wanted to speak with him about.

Me: Thanks for letting me know. I have a question, though.

I set my phone down, but it didn't take long for Troy to respond.

Troy: Is everything okay? Do I need to come see you?

Me: No, no. I'm okay. It's just ... would I be invading your space too much if I stayed one more night here?

I felt like a pathetic idiot sending that message. But I was glad I didn't have to wait long for a response.

Troy: I want you to save this text for when you're questioning yourself like this again. Sadie, you can stay at my place as long as you need. You can come to my place at any time. My space is yours. So, if you want one more night—or a million more nights—you've got it.

I smiled at his message.

Me: A million nights, huh? That's a lot of nights. I think you'd get sick of me by then.

Troy: Want to try me?

Me: Maybe some other time. But on a serious note? Thank you. Honestly. I really appreciate it. And I'll see you at class. I could definitely use a way to blow off some steam after today.

Troy: Do I even want to know?

Me: Let's just say writing articles isn't always the smoothest job in the world. Just a bunch of idiots making idiotic moves I then have to clean up.

Troy: Sounds like my day. Bunch of idiots doing idiot things with their money before I have to come in and save them.

Me: Sounds like you could use some time to blow off steam too.

Troy: Well, I look forward to seeing you in class. Gotta go. Another client is trying to call.

Me: Take a deep breath and don't wring their necks. That might not be a good look for your Yelp page.

I set my phone down and got back to work. But it felt as if a severe weight had been lifted off my shoulders. As much as I hated to admit it, I wasn't ready to go back home. Not tonight, anyway. And after shopping for a few outfits, I was ready for class. Especially since I wanted to try out this new ensemble Paris helped me pick out. I had new tennis shoes and new handguards. A tank top that apparently wicked sweat away and loose windbreaker shorts that would help with leg mobility in kickboxing class. I worked quickly through the rest of my day so I could get ready for class.

And right at six, I took my place near my sandbag.

"All right, class! Today, we're ramping it up a notch. If you need to rest and take a breather, do yourself a favor and do it. It's going to be a high-paced class today, tailored to work up a sweat and push your cardiovascular limits. Don't overdo it. This class isn't to come out on top. It's to push your top a bit further before knowing when to quit. Because both concepts are equally important."

Troy looked over at me, and somehow, I knew his statement was geared toward me more than anyone else. I didn't hate him for it, though. He had a good point. The music started and the warm-up began. And holy hell, he wasn't kidding. After the ten-minute warm-up, I was already dripping sweat.

But I didn't stop.

"Cross! Jab! Hook! Uppercut! Two kicks, jab. Come on, guys. It's not that hard of a pattern!"

I took out all my fear and all my anger on that fucking sandbag. It swung as I grunted and groaned out into the room. Our little corner filled with the smell of sweat quickly. Paris, dripping down her back. Uma, with her hair soaked and sticking to her forehead. And me, whose legs apparently dripped with sweat before any other part of my body did.

Odd.

"Cross, jab, hook, upper. Cross, jab, hook, upper. It's only going to get faster from here!" Troy exclaimed.

Half the class groaned before a few walked over to the sidelines. I kept up, though. I took things down a notch if I had to. Eliminated what I needed to instead of trying to come up from behind. But I didn't want to stop. It felt too good to move. It felt too good to be free again.

And when Troy finally said those magic words, most people fell on-to their backs.

"All right, class. Time for our cooldown. Sit down, hands above her head, lock your fingers, and breathe."

I, however, did exactly as he asked.

I heaved for air. I forced myself to feel the pain. To cope with it. To deal with it, even though my muscles burned. Even though my anger took hold. I let myself experience it instead of trying to fight it. I was tired of fighting. Tired of running. Tired of hiding all the damn time and thinking I wasn't worth shit. I closed my eyes and focused. I paid attention to my heart rate and how it slowly settled back into place. My legs created small puddles beneath me on the matted floors. But Paris had been right about this tank top.

It wicked away sweat from my torso like magic.

"Ready for some self-defense training?"

I slowly opened my eyes and found Troy sitting in front of me.

"Actually, I'm feeling pretty good right now," I said breathlessly.

"I don't think any of us can do anything right now anyway," Uma murmured.

"You kicked my ass." Paris groaned.

Troy grinned. "That was the point of the class."

I nodded. "I'm proud of myself. I didn't stop once. I mean, I dropped some moves and took the pace to half-time sometimes. But I didn't take a break."

He nodded. "I noticed that. I'm proud of you too. You've come a long way since you started these classes."

I smiled. "Feels good."

"You sure you don't want to learn any self-defense tricks today?"

I nodded. "I'm sure. I mean, the only reason why I didn't use them when Luke was in the house was because—"

I felt their eyes on me as memories washed over my mind. I felt myself tense. I felt myself already wanting to run from it. Run from the fear. Run from the pain. Run from the heartache. But I let myself experience it. I let myself feel it. I let it bury deep, crawling into the recesses of my soul and digging deep into my brain.

"You okay?" Troy asked.

I slowly nodded. "Maybe during the next self-defense class, we can center the moves around what to do if someone's got a weapon. Had he not had that weapon, I could've taken him down just fine. But that gun freaked me out. I didn't know what to do with that in play."

"That's exactly what we'll do, then," he said.

"Oh, have you guys looked into getting any security systems yet?" Paris asked.

"What?" Uma asked.

"Paris, I haven't talked with them about that yet," Troy said.

My hands fell into my lap. "Security systems?"

Paris sighed. "Well, Troy and I were talking over our lunch break, and we figured it might be smart to get one for the house now. You know, for you and Uma to have peace of mind."

Troy nodded. "And for the police to be alerted immediately if something like that ever happens again."

I looked over at Uma. "It's not a bad idea, honestly."

She shrugged. "I'm down if you're down."

Paris snickered. "See, Troy? Told you it wouldn't be an issue."

I furrowed my brow. "You thought it would be an issue?"

Troy sighed. "I said it *might* be an issue. Depending on whether or not you were ready to talk about that sort of thing. But it seems as if you're more willing to talk about it than I figured."

I nodded slowly. "I don't know. I just—"

I took my time to gather my thoughts before closing my eyes.

"All my life, I've been running. Not always a bad thing, but ... sometimes a bad thing. I have this nasty habit of running from emotions too. Feelings. Bad circumstances. I'm the kind of person who just compartmentalizes and keeps trucking, you know?"

"She really is," Uma said.

I opened my eyes. "But, if I'm ever going to get better, or stronger, or get through this at all, I have to process things. I have to let myself experience things, instead of running or stuffing it all away. So, that's what I'm trying to do. And not talking about things doesn't help. So, yeah. I'm talking about things. For now, at least."

Troy took my hand. "I'm so fucking proud of you, beautiful."

Paris sighed. "Awww, how adorable!"

Uma giggled. "The two of you are too much."

I rolled my eyes. "Thanks, you guys."

But when Troy squeezed my hand, I felt a small part of myself come alive. A part of me I thought was completely dead after all this nonsense.

"I'm not going to lie, though. A security system is a lot of money to upkeep monthly," I said.

"But, can you really put a price on being safe in your own home again?" Uma asked.

"I've got a guy I can talk to. He might be able to cut you a deal," Troy said.

I snickered. "You know guys everywhere, don't you?"

Paris laughed. "He really does. It's insane how networked he is with the community. Trust me, I'm sure he knows a guy who knows a guy who can buy you a tiger to put in an in-ground pool in your backyard."

I blinked. "Wait, you know a guy who knows a guy who can get someone a tiger?"

Troy grinned. "I guess you'll never know, unless you want a tiger."

Uma smiled. "Or an in-ground pool."

Paris butted in. "Do tigers swim? I'm not sure if they swim."

Troy shrugged. "Who says you have to fill up the pool? Just drop the tiger in it and—"

I held my hand up. "Okay, okay, okay. Yikes. I think we've gotten way off topic here."

Everyone shared a moment of laughter before I drew in a deep breath.

"There's a much more pressing issue here none of us are talking about," I said.

They all looked around at one another before their eyes came back to mine.

"What is it?" Paris asked.

"You okay?" Uma asked.

"What's going on?" Troy asked.

I sighed. "What the fuck are we doing for food?"

Our heads fell back in laughter before we all helped one another off the matted floor. After walking to a diner not too far up the road from the gym, we all decided to part ways. Uma went to stay with a nurse friend of hers, Paris headed to ... wherever it was she was headed, and me?

Well, I walked with Troy back to his place.

"Do you need anything?" he asked.

I watched him lock the door to his condo before he turned to face me.

"Thank you," I said.

He furrowed his brow. "For what?"

I walked over and stood toe-to-toe with him. My neck, craned back. My hands, finding his. I held his grip softly within mine before pulling him closer. And as his body heat wrapped around me, I stood on my tiptoes. Kissing his lips softly.

And I felt him tense.

"It's okay. You can kiss me," I whispered.

He growled softly as he pulled his hands from mine. He cloaked my back, pulling me closer to him as my arms slid around his neck. Our tongues fell together and my body came alive. I had missed this closeness with him. I had missed his embrace. The way his tongue always battled mine for control. For dominance. The way his muscles provided a foundation for the rest of my body. He picked me up. He walked me over to the couch. He sat me on the back of the couch as his hands settled in the dips of my waist.

Then, his forehead fell against mine as our eyes found each other.

"You're important to me, Sadie. And whatever you need—or don't need—is exactly what I'll give you. Okay?"

I smiled softly. "Thank you for understanding that. For understanding that things just—"

He cupped my cheek and my eyes fluttered closed.

"We're taking this at your pace. Whenever you're ready. Whatever you're ready for. I'm completely following your lead here. All right?"

I nodded softly. "Thank you so much."

"I'll wait as long as you need to in order to feel comfortable again."

Tears brewed behind my eyes. "You're amazing, you know that?"

He kissed the tip of my nose. "Not as amazing as you. But I do know one thing we both need."

My eyes fell open. "What's that?"

He grinned. "Showers. We both need showers."

"Are you telling me I stink, Troy?"

"Are you telling me I don't?"

I wrinkled my nose. "Good point."

He smiled. "I'll see you in the morning, okay? I should be up before you, so there will be coffee in the pot already."

"And food on a plate. I know how you operate now. You like to cook for others, don't you?"

"Eh, it's the small joys, I guess."

I kissed his lips softly. "You're one hell of a man, you know that?"

"Maybe you make me one. How about that?"

I snickered. "All right, all right. Shower time before both of us get way too mushy."

He helped me off the back of the couch. "Be as mushy as I can get. Noted."

I rolled my eyes. "You would."

"Good night, Sadie."

I stood there, gazing up at him. Taking in his features. His eyes. His muscles. The way he hovered over me, but didn't try to control me. The way he comforted me instead of making me feel fearful. I was a lucky woman, and I'd do whatever it took to keep a man like him in my life.

A man so completely opposite my ex.

"Good night, Troy," I said.

Then, we headed into our respective rooms to take showers.

And the entire time, I resisted the urge to go hop into Troy's shower with him.

Chapter 6

Troy

"So, I'll see you around twelve thirty for lunch?"

Sadie slid off my bike. "Yep. See you then. I think it's the taco truck today that's making its rounds."

"Oh. bless that damn taco truck."

She giggled, kissing my cheek. "You're insane. But I have to go. I'm about to be late."

"Go on. I'll see you in a few hours."

"Thanks for the ride, Troy!"

"Anytime!"

I grinned as she rushed inside to work. Then, I pulled away from the curb. I had a couple of errands I needed to run before I headed into work myself. And I wanted to make sure I got them out of the way. I stopped by the store and picked up a few more bottles of Sadie's favorite flavored waters. I grabbed a few snacks for us to share tonight. I also made sure to stock up on more pain medication. Since Sadie woke up very sore this morning from the class last night.

I felt good about things.

I mean, no. We weren't sleeping in the same bed or anything. We still had our separate spaces in my condo. But I enjoyed waking up to Sadie. I enjoyed making her breakfast in the mornings. I enjoyed sharing coffee with her before we had to set out for our days. It was a routine I had gotten used to. And I wasn't sure what I'd do once it went away.

Does it have to go away, though?

I got so lost in thought that I didn't see the person who came at me. One minute, I was daydreaming about living with Sadie, and the next? I was being wrenched off the damn sidewalk. The bag of medication from the pharmacy dropped to the ground. I felt a tight grip around my arm, causing me to act purely on instinct. I didn't know who the fuck was grabbing me like that, but they were about to learn their lesson.

And the instrument of instruction?

My mean right hook.

I felt my fists connecting with something solid. I felt an arm wrap around my neck and I quickly tossed the fucker over my shoulder. I dropped to the floor, kneeing the asshole in his gut as he gasped for air. And after delivering two massive blows to his face, I recognized who was below me.

Holy shit.

It was Luke.

With him struggling underneath me, I pulled out my cell phone. I dialed emergency immediately as his hands reached up for my neck. I rolled my eyes before punching him one last time. Square against his nose. And when he passed out against the concrete, I rattled off my location for the very kind woman on the other end of the line.

Then, I waited.

Everything happened so quickly. I heard sirens. I felt an officer pulling me away from Luke. Then, I watched them slap cuffs on the man bleeding from his nose. And his lip. And what looked like his ear.

"Sir, can you tell me what happened?"

The officer's voice pulled me from my trance and I smiled brightly.

"That man, who has an open case for domestic violence by the way, attacked me from out of nowhere. He pulled me into the alleyway and tried to take me down. I was only exerting my right to self-defense."

The man nodded. "That's what a couple of other witnesses have told my partner. There aren't any cameras in this alley. But, there are a few storefront cameras across the street. If we're lucky, they caught something."

"Does this mean I can press charges?"

"If you want, sir."

I grinned wildly. "I most certainly do want to press charges."

I stayed with the cops until they had hauled Luke away. I gave them all my information and told them I wanted to charge that man to the fullest extent I could. Then, I ripped my cell phone out of my pocket. I gathered up the bag of medication that had dropped to the ground, making my way back for my bike. And as I shoved everything into my storage compartment, my friend finally picked up.

"Troy! Long time, no talk. And if you're calling to bitch about me not riding lately, it's my back. It's acting up again."

I threw my leg over my bike. "I'm sorry to hear that, Duke. But I'm not calling because of your absence. I'm calling because someone I care about is in need of a very nice home security system."

"And you're wanting to cut her a deal."

"How did you know it was a—?"

"Troy, I've known you for years. You're a walking chivalrous asshole, if there ever was one. What's this girl gotten herself into this time?"

I watched the police cruiser cart off Luke as I drew in a deep breath.

"An abusive ex who burst into her home with a gun," I said.

"Oh, fuck. Hell yeah, I'll get you hooked up. I take it you want top tier?" he asked.

"That'd be appreciated. But the only requirements are something that can arm the doors and windows, something that requires a passcode to turn off the alarm, and something that alerts police if the passcode isn't entered within a certain time frame."

"I've got systems that come with verbal passwords too."

"The more security, the better."

After making the arrangements with Duke on the system, I headed into work. I knew I needed to call Sadie and tell her what happened. But I was still trying to wrap my head around things. Everything happened so quickly. In some respects, I still hadn't convinced myself it was real. I mean, Luke? Pulling me into an alley? What the fuck did he think he was going to accomplish? Beating me to a pulp like he probably thought he could do to Sadie? The man was delusional.

The man had been arrested.

Holy shit, the man was off the streets.

I pulled into my parking space at work and headed into my office. And the first phone call I placed was to Sadie. I sat in my office chair as her cell phone rang. And rang. And rang.

Then, she finally picked up.

"Troy, where are you?"

I blinked. "Where are you?"

"I'm headed out of work now. The police just called me. Apparently, Luke's been arrested. I'm headed to the police station now to ID him."

"That's what I was calling you about."

"Wait, how do you know Luke's been arrested?"

I stood up quickly. "Because I'm the reason he got arrested."

"You want to spit out *why* for me?"

I sighed. "Take a breath, Sadie. Everything's okay."

"Take a breath? Take a breath!? My ex has been arrested and you're telling me you're the reason and you want me to take a breath? What happened this morning, Troy? Tell me."

"I am. Just breathe. Everything is okay. Luke's off the streets."

"What did he do to you? Are you okay? Please don't tell me you're in the hosp—"

"Sadie!"

She paused. "Sorry. Yes. Uh, are you okay?"

I sighed. "I'm fine, Sadie. But, when you get to that police station, you're going to find him pretty beat up. I was running some errands this morning and he pulled me into an alleyway."

"Seems to be a trend for him," she murmured.

I snickered. "My instincts kicked into gear and he didn't stand a chance. I didn't even know who it was until he was already on the ground."

"What would make him do something like that, though? Clearly, he didn't think he could actually take you, right?"

I shrugged. "Desperate men get, well, desperate. There's no telling what he was thinking. I mean, for all I know, he had a weapon on him and simply didn't have time to get it out."

She paused. "Troy?"

I gathered my things. "You don't even have to ask. I'll meet you at the police station, all right?"

She sniffled. "Thank you. My cab just pulled up. I'll see you there."

"See you there, beautiful."

Apparently, the whirlwind of my day wasn't over yet.

As quickly as I had gotten into my office, I was gone. I struck up my bike and swerved through traffic, trying to make it downtown as quickly as possible. The police station was insanely crowded. I almost couldn't find a parking space in the overflow parking lot. But, once I got parked and got inside, I found Sadie sitting in a secondary waiting room. With her head bowed. And her hands clasped together.

And her legs jiggling up and down.

"Hey there," I said.

She whipped her head up as I sat down next to her.

"Troy," she said breathlessly.

I settled my hand over both of hers. "I'm here. It's okay. It's going to be okay. I need you to hear that."

Her gaze ran over my body. "Did he hurt you?"

I shook my head. "Didn't once get a knock in. I promise."

"He's such an idiot."

"Yes. Yes, he is."

I looked at the clock on the wall and almost burst out laughing. Ten in the morning. Holy fucking hell, all of this had happened before ten in the fucking morning. I shook my head while we sat there. As the minutes ticked over into hours. Sadie laid her head against my shoulder and I wrapped my arm around her. Keeping her warm in the ice-cold box the police station called a waiting room.

"Are you Sadie Powers?" an officer asked.

She shot up from my shoulder before she stood to her feet.

"I am, yes," she said.

"We're ready for you to make an identification," he said.

I hung back in the waiting room while she went to ID him. Then they pulled me into the same room to make the same identification. I smirked when I saw his bruised face. Tissues jammed up his nostrils. He looked like he had the brakes beat off him. And I was proud to have done that to such a massive womanizing asswipe.

"Yeah, that's him. That's the guy who tried to jump me this morning," I said.

"And you're sure about that," the officer said.

I smiled. "One hundred percent."

Sadie stood by my side as I filed my own charges against him for assault. Then, I stood by her while they updated the case she had open on him. By the time it was all said and done, it was nearly three in the afternoon. And the two of us were starving.

"You want to try a restaurant instead of the taco truck?" I asked.

Sadie nodded. "Yeah. That sounds good. You know, sitting down somewhere warm. Maybe sipping on some coffee?"

"Your wish is my command."

Chapter 7

Sadie

I didn't even know where to begin. The day had been so ... weird. Such a whirlwind of things that didn't make sense. From the moment I got the phone call from the police station, telling me Luke had been arrested, I had so many questions. So many things I wanted to ask. Wanted to know. But the only thing I knew I felt was relief.

Luke was finally behind bars.

Even as I ate a late lunch with Troy, I was shocked at my strength. How I didn't break down. How I didn't start crying. How I didn't lose my cool. I was more relieved than anything else. Because that meant I could stop looking over my shoulder. I could stop jumping at shadows in the night. I could stop sleeping with one eye open and wondering when he'd yank me from the streets again. Or press a gun to my side. Or generally get me cornered exactly how he wanted me.

I was proud of my strength.

And I knew it came from the confidence Troy's classes had given me.

"Do you want to talk about anything?"

His voice ripped me from my trance. "Actually, no."

He paused. "Are you sure?"

I nodded. "I know you're worried about me. But I promise you. I'm okay."

"I have to say, I'm a bit shocked at that. Not that I don't believe you. Just figured..."

"Yeah, me too."

"Yeah."

We finished up our dessert before Troy picked up the check. I didn't bother fighting him on it either. I knew he'd never let me pay for anything so long as he was around. The thought made me smile. Brightly, in fact. So much so that it hurt my cheeks.

"What's that for?" he asked.

"What's what for?" I asked.

"The smile. What are you thinking about?"

I reached for his hand. "You."

He took my hand. "I'm really glad you're feeling good about this. I was worried for you. Back there in the police station."

"I'm honestly just glad I can go home now."

"What?"

"I mean, you know. With Luke being held with no bond, there's nothing keeping me and Uma from going back to the house."

"This is true."

"Are you okay with that?" I asked.

He shrugged. "It's not something for me to be okay with or not be okay with."

"Troy."

"I talked to Duke. You know, that friend of mine?"

I grinned. "The tiger guy?"

He snickered. "No, the security system guy. He's willing to install one of the best security systems in your home for half the cost he usually charges, and the monthly service fee is only thirty-four bucks a month."

"That's actually pretty reasonable."

"I'd feel better about relinquishing you back to your home if you had it installed."

"Even with Luke off the streets?"

"Even so. That thing will protect you from more than just him. Please, get it installed. I'll pay the installation fee and you can—"

"Troy, I can take care of—"

"Let me pay the damn fee, Sadie."

I blinked. "Okay. Okay, yeah. You can pay it then."

He sighed. "I'm sorry. I just—"

I licked my lips. "You're worried."

He nodded slowly. "A bit, yeah."

"If it'll make you feel better, you can pay the installation fee and have it installed. Thirty-four bucks a month split between two people isn't that big of a deal. I actually figured it would be much more than that."

"Thank you. I appreciate that."

"And thank *you* for looking into that for me. For everything you've done for me, really."

We sat there in silence for a little while. Until the waiter came back with Troy's card and the receipt. He brought my hand to his lips to kiss before releasing me. Then, he signed on the dotted line before we got up to leave.

"Am I taking you back to work, or...?"

I sighed. "Actually, no. I told my boss I'd work from home the rest of the day. So, I should probably get my stuff from your place and make good on my word."

"So, my place to get your things and then ... home."

I nodded slowly. "Yep. Your place, then home."

Though, that didn't roll off the tip of my tongue as well as I figured it needed to.

I clung to him as we rode to his apartment. I packed up the things I had there, then he drove me back to my place. All the way out to Washington. And the drive seemed longer than normal. We pulled into the driveway and he helped me into the house. Helped me unpack my things in my room. Helped me clean up the place a bit. He even rubbed my back while I shot Uma a text message, letting her know I was back at the house and that things were safe again.

Then, I stood by the window and watched Troy ride off into the distance.

I stood there much longer than I anticipated. I watched the sun set. I watched darkness take over the sky. I even watched Uma pull up in her beat-up hatchback of a car. I stared out the window with my arms crossed tightly over my chest. Wondering what Troy was up to. Wondering what he was doing with his life right now.

And as Uma came into the house, she sighed.

"Troy not here?" she asked.

I shook my head slowly. "No."

"Why didn't he stay with you?"

I shrugged. "I didn't ask him to."

Uma tossed her keys into the bowl by the front door before coming over to me. She rubbed my back as we both stood at the window, gazing out into the front lawn. I felt lost. Like a buoy in the ocean, bobbing away without a boat to call home. Without a direction to lean toward. Surrounded by nothing but water and a great expanse I had no idea how to explore.

"You know, things like this happen more often than we like to admit. And when they do happen, people need to be surrounded by those they love."

I blinked slowly. "Gotcha."

"Call him, Sadie. Call all of them. Paris. That boy of hers she's seeing. Get them over here and surround yourself with people who care about you. It isn't weak to want a support system. However, it's cowardice to not admit when you do need them. And Luke was nothing but a coward. Don't be like him, Sadie. Be better."

I looked over at her. "I love you. You know that, right?"

She cupped my cheek. "I love you too. And just like everything else, we're going to get through this. Together. Okay?"

My eyes watered. "Okay."

She brought me in for a massive hug. A hug I desperately needed. I cried into her shoulder, letting out all the emotions I had been keeping inside for days. Weeks, really. My body shook. It felt as if I were spiraling out of control. But I forced myself to experience it and I didn't make myself stop crying.

"Call them," Uma whispered.

"Okay," I choked out.

An hour and a half later, the house was full of people again. Paris and Wren came over with drinks. Troy walked in with four massive pizzas. Uma and I got in the kitchen to cook up some cinnamon rolls and brownies. And together, we all sat down in the living room.

The evening was a blur. But, a good blur. We all told hilarious stories from our childhoods, and I gave them some great ammunition to use for later. I mentally went around every room of the house and told stories of great memories I had in each of them. Diving into my parents' bed every Christmas at five in the morning. Running around with friends in the backyard. My father hanging a rope climb on a massive tree in the backyard, only for me to work my hands to blisters trying to get up it.

It was an evening full of booze, pizza, and good memories.

And by the time I started yawning, my house felt like a home again.

Well, almost, anyway.

"Thank you, guys, so much for coming over," I said.

Paris hugged my neck. "You know I'm only a phone call away."

Wren nodded. "Yeah, and you have my number now. So, if you need anything—even if it's not personal—you can call. You got a friend in the department now. Use it, if you need to."

I smiled. "Thank you. I really appreciate that."

"You sure you don't need anything else?" Troy asked.

I reached out for him and took his hand.

"Actually, could you hang back for a bit?" I asked.

"Oh, sounds secretive," Paris said.

Troy nodded. "Of course. Whatever you need."

I ushered the guests out and waved them all off. Then, I headed back inside. I took Troy's hand again and tugged him toward the couch. Where we promptly flopped down. His arms fell around me. He pulled me in next to his body. I closed my eyes and sighed, sinking deeper into him. Enjoying his presence. Enjoying his scent. Enjoying the peace and quiet that came with the house as Uma shuffled her way into her bedroom.

"Troy?" I asked softly.

"Yeah?"

"Will you stay the night here with me?"

He hugged me tightly. "I'd love to."

"Thank you."

"Where do you want me to sleep?"

I paused. Shit. I hadn't thought that far ahead. I felt myself tensing and his hands started massaging. I sat up from his body and he scooted closer to me.

"Hey, hey, hey. It's okay. Don't panic," Troy said.

"I'm sorry. I just—uh, I hadn't thought that far—"

"I'll sleep on the couch," he said.

"That's such a shitty place to put someone who's done so much for me, though," I said breathlessly.

"I mean, are you comfortable enough with me sleeping in bed with you?"

I paused. "No. I'm sorry."

"Then, I'm on the couch, and it's not an issue. Okay?"

"I'm so sorry."

He cupped my cheek. "Hey, now. Don't be. You have nothing to be sorry for."

"I'm making you sleep on the couch, though."

"You're not making me do anything. I'm just glad you asked for what you wanted instead of burying it down. I'm proud of you, Sadie."

I smiled softly. "Really?"

He nodded. "Really. Now, it's time for both of us to get some sleep. It's been a hell of a day, and we both still have work tomorrow."

I sighed. "Yeah."

"So, get upstairs, get comfy, and get some rest. I'll be down here if you need me."

Reluctantly, I got off the couch. I kept peeking back at Troy, watching as he tried to get comfortable on the couch. He threw the back cushions to the floor and slid off his jacket. He slung his leg over the back of the couch and shifted around to either side. I felt like shit, having him sleep on that thing. There was no way in hell he'd ever get comfortable on something like that.

So, when I heard him pacing downstairs, I decided it was time to suck it up.

"Troy?" I asked.

I walked to the top of the steps and saw him staring up at me.

"Are you okay, Sadie?"

I shook my head. "No. I'm not."

He rushed up the stairs as his hands cupped my cheeks.

"What's wrong? Talk to me," he said.

I smiled softly. "No funny business. I'm not ready for that yet. But, you can't sleep on that couch. And, I wouldn't mind a cuddle buddy. If that's all right."

He grinned. "Of course, that's all right."

"Good. Okay. Come on. I think my bed's a bit more comfortable than that couch."

"A bed full of nails is more comfortable than that couch."

I barked with laughter. "We need a new couch. Got it."

All night long, I slept in Troy's embrace. Wrapped around him. Feeling him pull me close every time I shifted. And the safety I felt in his embrace went unmatched. I'd never felt that safe before. Ever. And I knew no damn security system would ever replicate that feeling. I slept better than I had in days.

And when I woke up to his smile the next morning, my heart skipped a beat.

I could get used to this.

I wouldn't mind getting used to it either.

Chapter 8

Troy

Sadie: I hope you're having a good day. I wanted to let you know that I've gotten my information for my trip to Florida. I leave early in the morning for a couple of days. Want to come over for dinner tonight? My treat.

I read over her message a few times. I don't know why, but I already missed her. I knew how excited she was to have her travel privileges for work reinstated. Especially after all the chaos. But, I worried she wasn't ready for something like that yet.

Plus, I didn't want her to be so far away.

Me: Sounds good. What time would you like me over?

I watched those three little dots bounce around on my screen, and it made me smile. Because on the other side of that phone she was sitting somewhere. Being the most beautiful woman in the world. Waiting for me to message. Waiting for me to speak with her.

Sadie: How does six thirty sound?

Me: I'll see you then, beautiful. Don't miss me too much.

Sadie: Too late.

A bright smile spread across my face before my trance was interrupted.

"What's got you smiling like a schoolgirl this morning?" Wren asked.

I turned off the screen of my phone and looked up to see him sliding into the booth. I shoved my phone into my pocket as our waitress came over, setting down a coffee mug for him. She filled up both of ours, set down a handful of creamers, then silently went on her way.

Dealing with everything from crying children who wanted pancakes instead of waffles and ornery old men who wanted their eggs sunny-side up with soft yolks instead of hard ones.

"Earth to Troy. You there, dude?" Wren asked.

I cleared my throat. "Sorry. Long night."

"With Sadie?"

His grin made me snicker.

"No, asshole. If anything, it was my first night away from her since all this shit went down. Can't say I was too happy about not being closer to her," I said.

"Well, I'm sure she made it through the night. Right?"

I rolled my eyes. "Yeah, yeah. She's fine."

"So, the real issue is that you weren't close enough to protect her if something did happen."

"Yes, Dr. Wren."

He chuckled. "Hey, don't get pissed at me for the truth. Not my truth."

I sipped my coffee. "So, how much do you know already?"

"Eh, not much actually. Paris told me something about Luke being arrested. Said he beat you up or something?"

I snickered. "He tried beating me up. The idiot pulled me into an alleyway."

"Seems to be his MO."

"Right? Yeah. He just snatched me right off the damn street and I flew off my rocker on instinct. I didn't even know who the hell it was until after I swung my first couple of punches."

"Are you pressing charges?"

"Hell, yeah, I'm pressing charges. He's being held without bond until his arraignment. So, for now, he can't get to Sadie."

"Or you."

I shook my head. "I'm not concerned about me."

"Well, I am, dude. I'm very concerned about you. The guy's getting ballsy, going after you."

"And now, he can't go anywhere. Between the charges I have on him and the open case he has with Sadie, that fucker's going nowhere. I'm sure of it."

"Still, you should lawyer up. Just in case."

I nodded. "Already taken care of."

He leaned back in his seat. "Good."

I took another pull from my coffee. "So, I'm still trying to pick out the best security system for Sadie's home."

"You're still on that? I figured it would've already been installed by now."

"It's only been a couple of days."

"Since when have you ever moved that slowly with something relating to this girl."

I shot him a glare. "Asshole."

He chuckled. "Again, don't shoot the messenger."

I sighed. "I just want to make sure she gets the best bang for her buck. I'm weighing the pros and cons of everything before I choose a system."

"Well, when you're done? Send Duke my way. I think getting a small one installed at Paris's place might be nice."

I paused. "Has something happened?"

He shook his head. "No, nothing's happened. But I guess this shit with Sadie's got me thinking. You know, especially whenever I go over to Paris's place. She's, like, right smack-dab in one of the worst parts of this city. I've got no clue how she feels safe there."

"You and me both."

"Anyway, I think I might try to talk her into getting a security system. Even if it's just a basic one. You know, something to give me peace of mind."

I grinned. "Look at the two of us. Trying to protect our girls."

Wren smiled. "Yeah, and you know what happens when girls enter the picture."

I snickered. "We need to get some long rides on the schedule."

"You're damn right, we do."

"We should make some time to see the club too. We missed the fundraiser and that barbecue sale."

"Yeah, that shit blew by us without a second thought."

"And I'm sure the president is gonna want to chew our ear off about it."

He chuckled. "Might as well get it out of the way, huh?"

"You up for a ride Monday or Tuesday? After work?"

He shrugged. "Who's to say we can't do both?"

I grinned. "I like your style."

Wren and I sat and had coffee before devouring way too much breakfast food. And after we were done, we parted ways. I needed to get to the gym anyway. Mom needed some help around the place. Usually, Sundays were the days I had off. But, I needed to do something. I needed to get out of my condo. I needed to get my mind off things.

So, mindless cleaning at the gym seemed like a good way to go about it.

I walked from the diner to the gym and breathed in the fresh air. Reveled in the fact that no one passing by me was Luke. That fucking asshat. I unlocked the front doors of the gym and made my way to my office, flicking on lights as I went by. It was obvious Mom hadn't made it in yet. So, it was a good thing I decided to make it a workday today.

Because the gym was supposed to be open in ten minutes.

"Troy?"

Paris's voice caught me by surprise and I whipped around.

"What are you doing here on a Sunday?" she asked.

I shrugged. "Just getting a bit of work out of the way. Why? What's up?"

"I don't know. Maybe the fact that you never come in on Sundays to work."

I furrowed my brow. "I came in last Sunday to work."

"Well, other than that."

"I also came in three Sundays ago to—"

She held up her hand. "Point taken. I haven't had enough coffee for this."

"Should've grabbed breakfast with me and your boyfriend this morning. We had plenty of coffee to go around."

"Ah, no wonder there's no coffee. The two of you drained the entire city of its supply."

I chuckled. "I'll go put on some coffee in the lounge."

"And while you're at it, you can throw a load of those fluffy white towels in the washer. Your mother's been jumping down my throat about it because I apparently 'don't do them right.'"

"Sounds like her."

"I'll take that as a 'Yes, Paris; right away, Paris.'"

I shook my head before unlocking my office. I had some things I wanted to get out of the way for prospective clients. But first? Coffee for Paris. She was a miserable human being before coffee. And no one else needed to suffer her sarcastic wrath. I made my way to the lounge, grabbing massive rolling carts of sweat-stained towels in the process.

Then, I set about making the best pot of damn coffee this gym had ever smelled.

As I rolled the towels back toward the laundry room, I fell into the monotony of things. I ran through self-defense moves in my head that Wren and I could use for our next class. And I thought about how well Sadie kept up in kickboxing a few days ago. I mean, she kicked some serious ass. In my eyes, she was almost ready to move up in class. She was almost ready to start taking the intermediate kickboxing courses I taught at the gym as well.

Which meant I'd see her more often during the week. Since the intermediate classes weren't on the same days as the self-defense classes.

I dumped in some fabric softener before the detergent. And after running the towels on a hot washing load, I ran them through again. Only this time, it was a hot soak. That's what made towels fluffy. Washing them with a bunch of fabric softener, then soaking them and rinsing them again with nothing in the load. I cleaned up the laundry room and storage cabinets while I waited for them to cycle through. Then, I tossed the towels into the dryer on high heat.

Before seeking out the other three massive rolling carts we had stowed around the gym.

Sundays were always our slow days at the gym. But, this Sunday seemed particularly slow. I only ever saw four people in the gyms at a time. And there were so few people working up a sweat that I didn't even smell it. There was no grunting to be heard from the free-weight room. No dribbling sound of a basketball across the court. It was odd, seeing the gym this way. Taking it all in this way.

It made me wonder about what we could do to ramp up the activity in this place on a Sunday.

"Troy?"

I turned around at the sound of Mom's voice. "Hey there."

"What are you doing here?"

I shrugged. "Just needed to get out a bit. Plus, got a lot of emails and shit from clients. Figured I'd focus better on them in my office."

"Then, why are you in the laundry room?"

I thumbed over my shoulder. "Apparently, Paris doesn't do them right?"

She giggled. "So, instead of simply following the written instructions I gave her, she asks you to do it?"

"I mean, she wasn't caffeinated when she came in. So..."

"Yikes. Well, leave that load alone. I'll walk Paris through exactly how this needs to happen. She needs to learn. It's going to be part of her new job."

"New job?"

Mom grinned. "I've been thinking about promoting her to general manager of this place."

I smiled brightly. "That's a bold move. You think she'll take it?"

"I don't think there's anyone else half as dedicated to this gym as we are, except for her. And let's face it, we need a manager. You and I are too busy advertising, coming up with new things, teaching classes, and having equipment maintenanced to really manage the way it needs to be."

"You know that's a salaried position, right?"

She nodded. "With benefits. I'm already working out the logistics of everything. But, if she's going to take on the job, she has to learn how to do shit like this right instead of pawning it off on you. I swear, you bail her out more than your own damn self."

I chuckled. "Do you really expect anything different, though?"

"I stopped expecting anything but antics from the two of you a long time ago. Now, come on. Shoo. Go get Paris and tell her to get her ass in here."

"You want me to use those exact words, or...?"

"Shoo!"

Mom swatted at me and I laughed as I rushed out of the laundry room. I heard Paris whistling down the hallway, and I knew I was about to burst her fucking bubble. I made my way to the front desk and leaned against it. I stared at Paris, waiting for her to look up at me while she stared at the computer screen.

"Speak, or leave," she said.

"Not enough coffee yet?" I asked.

"There's never enough coffee when Wren's involved."

The grin on her face made me grimace.

"Yikes. No. Okay. Mom wants you in the laundry room, pronto."

She sighed. "Really?"

I nodded. "Really."

"I mean, come on. I'm working the front desk. What if a customer comes in or something?"

I turned around and looked out the door. Toward the empty parking lot. Searching for any sign of life before I turned back around and smiled.

"I'm sure I can handle the full breadth of people charging this front desk right now," I said coyly.

She stood up. "I hate you."

"Just listen to what Mom's telling you to do."

"She's insane. You know that, right?"

I nodded. "Yep. Lived my whole life with her. It won't change how she wants those towels washed, though."

"I don't have time to stand there and wait for them!"

You will as GM. "Just do as she asks, please. Don't ruin this for yourself."

"Ruin what?"

I grinned. "If you simply listen to Mom and stop pitching fits about the laundry, you'll figure it out."

She narrowed her eyes. "What do you know, Troy?"

"I know exactly what you know if you go in there and listen to Mom."

She sighed. "Fine, fine. I'll go in there and watch her run the towels through two different loads of washing shit before drying them. All the while, standing there and twiddling my thumbs."

"Actually, the second cycle of washing doesn't actually wash. It just rinses. You don't put anything in it."

"I'm going to dump my coffee on you."

I grinned. "Gotta catch me first."

And as I took off running toward my office, I heard Paris yelling behind me.

"You're just as bad as her, Troy!"

Sometimes, pissing that woman off gave me a good laugh.

Chapter 9

Sadie

"So, do I need to be scarce tonight?" Uma asked.

She nudged my shoulder as I stirred the meat sauce on the stove.

"Uma, I love you. But, if Troy and I have sex? We'll do it with you here, or without you here."

She paused. "I don't know whether to clap or be grossed out."

"Oh, come on. It's no different from you bringing home guys or whatever when we lived back in the apartment. I mean, I could only hear a *little* bit of what you guys were doing."

"Wait, what? You never told me that."

I giggled. "I'm just kidding. I'm pulling your leg. Settle down. It's fine."

She sighed. "You had me worried there for a second."

I paused. "What were you worried about me finding out?"

"None of your damn business, that's what."

I turned toward her. "What do you do in your spare time, you little freaky-deek."

"Nothing I'm going to be telling you now."

I smiled. "Well, maybe someday I'll tell you all of my and Troy's salacious little secrets."

"Yeah, if I don't hear them first."

"Oh, come on. We've got an entire floor separating us and we're on opposite sides of the house. You're not going to hear a thing. And that's if there's anything to hear tonight."

"Well, I think you should cut the guy—and yourself—some slack. You need to blow off steam. Especially before you get back in the air in the morning for work. Let loose, would ya?"

"I'll think about it. How's that sound?"

Uma helped me throw together a nice dinner for myself and Troy. Well, with the added bonus of making herself a massive plate for her own consumption. Fresh garlic bread, a massive tossed salad, home-made ranch dressing, and bow-tie pasta with meat-and-vegetable sauce. It all smelled amazing, and I couldn't wait for six thirty to roll around. I set the table while Uma made herself a plate. Then, I placed all the food on the table before grabbing some drinks.

"I'll be in my room if you two need me," she said.

"Thank you so much for your help. I really appreciate it," I said.

"You can thank me by blowing off some steam tonight, girl!"

And as she disappeared down the hallway, a knock came at the door.

Troy.

I smoothed my hands down my dress before opening the door. I smiled up at him before he pulled me in for a massive hug. I giggled as he picked me up, swinging me around in his embrace. And as he walked me back into the house, he kicked the front door closed.

Before kissing my cheek hard.

"Oh, I missed you today," he said.

I kissed his lips softly. "I missed you too."

"Mmm, something smells good in here."

"Uma and I made our version of pasta."

"I ... don't think it's the pasta I'm smelling."

His hands drifted down my body and I felt my cheeks heating. His lips captured mine for a searing kiss, but I felt a wave of panic rush over me. I gripped his wrists and slowly pulled them away from my body. I broke away from the kiss abruptly. I giggled to try and diffuse the tension, but I saw the concern in Troy's eyes.

"Too soon. I'm sorry. I should've—"

"No, no, no. It's fine. Really."

"Sadie, I didn't mean t—"

I took his hands in mine. "Just come eat. I know you've got to be starving, yeah?"

He nodded. "A bit, yes."

We sat down for dinner, but we didn't do much talking. This definitely wasn't the dinner I wanted to say goodbye on either. I mean, I knew I'd only be gone for a couple of days. But I'd miss him while I was in Florida. A lot. I wanted this dinner to be special. I wanted it to be magical. I wanted it to be so wonderful that it held us over for a couple of days until I got back into town.

The tension between us was palpable, though.

And not the good kind.

"So, I've been thinking," Troy said.

I set my spoon down. "About what?"

He leaned back in his chair. "About moving you up to the intermediate kickboxing class."

Why do I feel disappointed? "Oh."

"Oh?"

"I mean, just—not what I thought you were going to say."

"What did you think I was going to say?"

That you can't wait a second longer for me to make the first move.

"I don't know," I said.

He narrowed his eyes. "Sadie, if something's on your mind—"

"Why move me up?" I asked quickly.

He sighed. "Sadie."

"Why do you want to move me up? Because I'm a bit apprehensive about that. I haven't been taking classes long. And Uma isn't ready for that kind of move."

"I heard that!" she yelled down the hallway.

Troy and I laughed with each other before I stood from the table. Beginning the work to gather up my dirty dishes.

"Here, let me help," he said.

"Do you really think I'm ready for something like that?" I asked.

Troy followed me to the sink. "I really think you are. But, it's completely your decision. The intermediate classes aren't on the same days as self-defense, though. So, that's another issue to contend with."

I put my dishes in the sink. "What days and times are they?"

"Tuesday and Friday nights, same time. Six thirty."

I nodded slowly. "I'll definitely have to think about that."

"Just consider it. It's not a requirement. But I just wanted to let you know that you're ready. If you ever want to make that kind of a shift."

I smiled softly. "I appreciate that. Thank you, Troy."

"No problem."

He helped me put the leftovers away and clear the rest of the dishes. But once we were done, silence filled the space around us. I didn't know what to say. I didn't know what to think. However, when I looked up into his eyes, I knew what I wanted to *do*.

Even if my body was frightened.

"Troy?"

"Yeah?"

"Will you—?"

His hand cupped my cheek. "Take your time. We have all night."

I smiled softly. "Will you come upstairs with me?"

He searched my eyes. "You sure about that?"

I nodded. "Yeah. I'm sure."

"Because we don't have t—"

I fisted his shirt and pulled him down to me. I captured his lips with my own, wanting nothing more than to taste him. I knew if something didn't happen, I'd chicken out. I knew that if I didn't make some sort of move, I'd let Luke continue to ruin this for me. Continue to rob me of something meant to be so beautiful in my life. And I wouldn't let him control me like that any longer.

It was time for me to stop being scared.

"Fuck." Troy growled.

"Take me upstairs," I whispered.

His hands gripped my ass cheeks. He picked me up and carried me out of the kitchen. Over to the stairs. And up to the second floor. I reached out and closed my bedroom door just as we breached its threshold, my tongue unable to devour any more of him. I sucked on his lower lip. Our teeth clattered together. I felt my pussy wetting itself and I felt my thighs warming. I was ready for him. Ready for his intrusion.

"I've missed you so much." I breathed.

We collapsed to my bed and his hands wandered over my body. He pushed my dress up, my skin puckering at his touch. My nipples hardened against my bra. His lips kissed down my neck. Sucking, and nibbling, and licking his way down.

Down my breasts.

Down my stomach.

Down between my legs.

"Troy." I moaned.

"I'm ready for dessert." He grunted.

"Please. Please. I ... I ... I ... I need—"

He knelt between my legs and slid my panties off to the side. And the second his tongue hit my clit, my back arched. Electricity shot through my body, sizzling me to my core. I slid my legs over his shoulders. I gripped my thighs around his face. He lapped me, from slit to swollen nub, making me quiver and quake for him. His hands pinned my hips down. His growls pushed me further up that mountain. And as I bucked ravenously against his face, I found my end on the tip of his tongue.

"Troy! I'm coming!"

My body caved as he swallowed down my juices. Every last drop I had for him. His hands moved up my body, massaging my clothed breasts and tugging at my puckered nipples. I gasped for air. My eyes rolled into the back of my head. His tongue's assault didn't stop. Not once. Not giving me a second to breathe. I came down from my first high and ground myself against his face. Needy for more. Greedy for another one.

The headiness of his command called to me.

And I never wanted to lose this with him again.

"Yes. Yes. Yes. Yes."

"Come for me, Sadie. I know you have it in you."

"Oh, Troy. Oh yes. Oh, fuck. Oh, this feels so good."

"Mmm, yeah."

His tongue splayed out over my clit as he slipped a finger inside me. One, then two. Crooking them and stroking my inner walls. My eyes shot open. My jaw unhinged. My toes curled as my thighs clamped around his face again. And I fell over the edge. I tried calling out his name, but the pleasure was too great. I tried chanting his name, but I didn't have any breath to give. My back collapsed against the bed as my arousal dripped down my ass crack. I felt him cleaning me up, humming over my taste and enjoying every second of it.

Then, he kissed back up my body until our lips connected once more.

"I need you," I whispered.

My eyes found his and he nuzzled my nose. He rolled me onto my side, and I let him do it. I let him manipulate my body. I felt so weak from the pleasure he crashed over my system that I didn't know if I could move on my own or not. But, it didn't take me long to get what I wanted. To get what I needed from him.

Because once I heard the zipper of his jeans come undone, a sloppy smile crossed my face.

He pulled my leg back over his. With my back against his chest, he kissed my shoulder. My neck. The shell of my ear. He opened my body up, stretching my leg back as the tip of his dick found my entrance. And when he slowly slid inside, I pressed against him. Hard. Until our bodies were connected at the hips and I felt the beating of his heart between my shoulder blades.

"Like this?" he murmured.

I nodded. "Just like that. Oh, Troy. Just like that."

He moved with a languid pace I didn't think was possible for him. His hands explored my body, touching and caressing every inch. He snaked his hands underneath my clothing. He cradled my body against his. My walls clamped down around him, ready to pull him over the edge with me as his fingertips slid between my pussy folds. He worked my clit softly. Slowly. Tracing its outline as I whispered for more. He nibbled at the nape of my neck. He left soft bite marks against my shoulders. And as his cock grew against my walls, his fingers moved faster.

Quicker.

Harder.

Until I bucked back into him and lost myself in our heat.

"Yes. Fuck. Troy, I need you t—"

"Squeeze that cock, beautiful."

"Faster."

"That's it, Sadie. Tell me what you want."

"Harder, Troy. Please."

"There is it. I feel you squeezing. You want me to come, don't you?"

"Yes."

"You want me to say your name, don't you?"

I groaned. "Oh, yes."

He bit softly against the shell of my ear. "You want me to fill you all the way up, don't you?"

I ground my ass against his pelvis. "Fill me up. Please. Troy. I've missed you. Please. I'm so sorry. Please. Please. Please."

"You have nothing to be sorry for." He growled.

Then, his fingers pressed against my clit.

"Shit!"

I fell over the edge once more, my pussy clamping around his cock. I felt my body milking him. Massaging him. Wanting nothing more than to suck him dry. He rutted against me. Short, shallow thrusts. Timed perfectly with the collapsing of my walls as he fucked me through my pleasure. I reached back for his hair. I gripped it tightly, shoving his face into my neck. And as he sucked hard against my skin, I felt his dick pulse once. Twice. Three times.

Before his body shook against my own.

"Fuck." He grunted.

With every hot thread of arousal, I gasped for air. With every grunt against my skin, I shivered. I clung to him for dear life, refusing to let him go. Fearful that if I did, this would all be just a dream. He wrapped his arms around me. He collapsed against the bed. And as he held me in his arms, kissing the mark he left on my shoulder, I panted hard for air.

"You have to promise to call me and check in with me in the mornings and in the evenings," he murmured.

My eyes slowly fell open. "Huh?"

"While you're gone. Promise to check in with me. Every morning, and every night."

I nodded slowly. "Whatever you want."

"I want you to be safe, Sadie. That's what I want."

I turned around in his arms, feeling his cock fall away from my body. I scooted close to him, taking in the sweat on his brow. The way his cheeks were flushed. His disheveled hair and the worry that rushed behind his eyes. I captured his lips softly. I pulled him on top of my body. Then, as I locked my arms around his neck, I gazed into his eyes.

"I promise you, I'll check in," I said.

"That's all I ask."

Chapter 10

Troy

Sadie: I know this isn't a phone call, but I wanted you to know I just landed. I'll call you once I get checked into my hotel room. Kisses.

I grinned at the text before I set my phone off to the side. But, it wasn't long before my phone started ringing.

And her name scrolled across the screen of my phone.

"I take it you're at the hotel?" I asked.

"I am," she said breathlessly.

"You okay? You sound out of breath."

"Yeah, well. Elevator's busted in the hotel. And seven flights of steps with luggage is brutal. Even with my training."

I grimaced. "I'm sorry. When do they think they'll have it fixed?"

"Not while I'm here, that's for sure."

"Do you have any time to snag a nap before you have to start working?"

"That's the plan. But, I wanted to check in. I'm having dinner with my parents tonight, so I'm not sure what time I'm going to call. But, I'll definitely text."

I nodded. "Sounds good. Get some rest, beautiful."

"You have a good day at work too. Okay?"

"It'll be better now that I've heard from you."

She giggled. "You're too cute. Night, handsome."

I chuckled. "Sleep well."

She hung up the phone and I sat there for a few more seconds. Waiting for that dial tone. I don't know why I did. It was an odd thing to do. I guess ... I just really wanted to make sure she had hung up and not done anything else. Like put me on hold, or needed me to listen in on something.

It sounded like the weirdest thing in the world. But, I'd rather be on the phone too long after she hung up than hang up prematurely.

You're going insane, Troy.

The day crawled by. Every time I thought an hour had passed, it had only been fifteen minutes. It was a grueling day. And when five o'clock rolled around, I was happy to exchange my suit and tie for my leather jacket. I heard Wren's bike drive into the parking lot of the gym just as I pulled my coat over my shoulders. Paris tossed me a clipboard with some paperwork needing my signature. Then, I slapped it back down onto her desk.

"Don't wait up," I said.

She shook her head. "You're relentless. I'm telling Sadie on you!"

"If you speak to her, tell her she still has yet to call me tonight!"

I headed out the front doors of the gym and hopped on my bike. With the sun beating down against my back, I fell in line beside Wren as we sped off into the late afternoon. We weaved in and out of traffic. We blazed through yellow lights and went down some of our favorite back roads. The tight corners always gave me an adrenaline rush. A bit of drifting. A bit of burned rubber. A bit of smoke being left behind us. It made me feel free. It made me feel powerful. It made me feel alive.

Not quite as free, powerful, and alive as Sadie.

But it came close.

I followed Wren out of the city, tracing our familiar highway pattern toward the water's edge. With the sun at our backs and the smell of water lacing our nostrils, I felt more relaxed than I had in days. All this worrying over Sadie had me locked up with tension. And while I wouldn't trade it for anything in the world, it felt nice to relax.

Especially once I heard my built-in Bluetooth phone ringing in my helmet.

"This is Troy," I said as I answered the call.

"Wow, those are some sounds. What are you doing?" Sadie asked.

I grinned. "Hey there, beautiful."

"Are you on your bike?"

"I've got a Bluetooth thing in my helmet. Don't worry, hands-free, and all that."

"Well, it better be. Otherwise, I'd have to bitch you out for not staying safe so you can keep me safe."

I chuckled. "I bet you're cute when you're angry."

"But you won't find that out, because you're a good boy. Right?"

I paused. "Are you patronizing me?"

"It's bad if you have to question that."

"And here I thought I was the one with jokes."

She giggled. "Well, I wanted to call and check in before dinner because my parents are apparently keeping me out all night."

I sped to catch up with Wren. "Sounds like fun. What's the plan?"

"Well, dinner. Then, coffee and dessert. And then, there's this bar-club thing around here that they go to. Apparently. There's this cover band they enjoy, and they want me to sit and listen to a few songs. They said for me to plan on 'partying as if I were back in college.'"

"Did you even party in college?"

"Nope."

I barked with laughter. "Well, it does sound like a good time."

"Do you want me to message you when I get in for the night?"

"Not if you're too tired. If you're going to be with your parents, that's good enough for me. Just make sure someone knows you got up to the hotel room safely after. All right?"

Wren and I took the exit for the lake and I saw the water's edge coming into view.

"All right. We'll talk in the morning, then?" Sadie asked.

"I'm looking forward to it. You have fun with your parents, okay?" I asked.

"I will. I promise."

"Good girl."

"Hey, now you're patronizing me."

"Not one bit."

She giggled. "Talk to you tomorrow, Troy."

"Until tomorrow, beautiful."

I cut the call just as we drove up to the throng of bikes already in the parking lot. I looked over at Wren as he pulled his helmet off, wondering what the hell he had gotten us into. I took off my own helmet and turned off my bike. And it wasn't until I saw who was parked with us that I smiled.

"Finally. You two assholes show back up," the president said.

"Hey there, man," I said.

I put the kickstand down on my bike and he came to clap me on the back. Wren and I hugged the guys before heading over to the taco truck. Wren must've arranged this. Because the guys never rode out this far. It wasn't their "territory," so to speak.

"So, what gives with you guys being out here?" I asked.

Wren snickered. "Apparently, your girl's article did exactly what it needed to do."

I blinked. "What?"

The president chuckled. "Yeah. Seems a piece on old Joe's there made it into the paper. Ranting and raving about wings and fries and shit."

Wren smiled. "Our poor dive bar isn't quite a dive bar any longer."

I rolled my lips over my teeth to keep from laughing.

"I mean, good for them? For the business?" I asked.

"Yeah, yeah. Well, Wren here called me yesterday and had some bright idea for us to cruise out to the water. Eat out of some taco truck," the president said.

"Doesn't sound like you're too keen on the idea of making this a regular thing," I said.

He shrugged. "Depends. How good are the tacos?"

I grinned. "You'll never look at another taco the same way once you've had one of theirs."

Wren clapped his hand on my shoulder. "Come on. My treat. Who's hungry."

The president narrowed his eyes. "Actually, I'm more interested in why we haven't seen you two around lately."

The guys murmured and nodded as I looked over at Wren.

"We've been ... a bit busy," I said.

"Yeah, with classes and such at the gym," Wren said.

"You missed the fundraiser," the president said.

"And the barbecue sale."

"And the last five rides."

A small uproar with the guys started growing and I knew I'd have to do something to calm them down. Especially if I wanted to preserve the integrity of this new spot of ours. I held up my hand to silence them. But, it wasn't until our president held up his own hand that the rest of the guys quieted down.

I didn't feel it was my place to tell Sadie's story to someone she didn't know.

But, I could talk around it.

"The girl I'm seeing—you know, who wrote that article?—has been going through a hard time right now," I said.

"Bad breakup and all," Wren said.

I shot him a look and he held up his hands in mock surrender.

"Anyway, I've been kind of throwing my energy into helping her. Making sure she's okay. Making sure she can ... take *care* of herself."

My eyes locked with the president and he nodded slowly.

"Uh-huh. And how's all of that going?" he asked.

"It's ... going. Getting better. Especially now that this bad breakup has..."

I looked over at Wren and he shrugged.

"Taken a turn for the better?" he asked.

"Something like that," I said.

The president's eyes bounced between us before he cleared his throat.

"Well, sounds like you two have had a lot on your plates," he said.

"It's been a journey, to say the least," I said.

"If there's anything you need—anything you need *us* to take care of—you let us know. Okay?"

I grinned. "Trust me, I know."

"And if this girl you're seeing ever wants someone to talk to about this kind of thing, you know my wife's—"

I cut him off. "That is more than generous. And I really do appreciate it. I'll let her know. You know, if she wants to talk to someone who gets it."

The president placed both of his hands on my shoulders.

"Good to have you two back," he said with a grin, "but I need some fucking food."

"Well, then quit with the princess-bonding moment and let's get some damn tacos!" I exclaimed.

And as the guys made their way to the truck, I looked over at Wren. He winked at me and I shook my head, watching as the guys bombarded that poor truck. The look on the woman's face as twelve bearded, bald, tattooed, and leather-wearing men rushed her ordering window was one I'd never forget. But, it only came in second to the face our president made when he bit into his first taco.

"Oh, hell yes. We're coming here every Monday for our rides," he said.

"Monday?" I asked.

Wren chuckled. "I might've talked him into changing the night of our group rides so we can cash in on the weekly treat."

I wrapped my arm around his shoulder. "You know how to work that magic of yours in the shadows, don't you?"

"I mean, you could've just asked Paris that."

I glared at him. "Don't make me drown you in this lake."

He threw his head back in laughter. "Come on, hangry. Let's get you some food before half the damn town goes missing."

Then, the two of us headed for the truck. Putting in our normal orders before laughing our asses off with the guys.

While they pressured the owner of the truck to start selling beer along with their tacos.

Chapter 11

Sadie

"So, how was the thing, honey?" Mom asked.

"The thing?" Dad asked.

I giggled. "It's okay. I can't actually talk about the thing until my article comes out. Can't have anyone talking about any sneak peeks anywhere," I said.

"Fine by me. I'm ready to tell you about our surprise anyway," Dad said.

"Your father is definitely a sneak peek kind of guy," Mom said flatly.

"Oh, come on. We were going to tell her in a few minutes anyway. We all have to leave to get on a plane in three hours," Dad said.

I paused. "We?"

As I sat with my parents at breakfast, I set my coffee down on the table. The hotel the Detroit Metro Times put me up in had been really nice. And my parents had met me for breakfast every single morning. Spending time with them had been outstanding. Much needed, especially after all the chaos my life had been through these past few weeks.

"Mom? Dad?" I asked.

"Well, sweetie..." Mom said.

"Your mother and I have decided to fly back with you for a few days," Dad said.

My jaw dropped open. "Wait, really?"

Mom nodded. "Yeah! I mean, we know Uma's staying in the house too. But, there's still that guest bedroom."

"And if you put a bed in the basement, we can sleep there too," Dad said.

"And if we come, we can stack the kitchen with groceries," Mom said.

"And I can start pulling up dead weeds I know no one's touched—"

I squealed, interrupting my father. I shot up from my chair and wrapped my arms around his neck, hugging him tightly. He stood up and held me close. In that fatherly bear hug of his I'd grown up with. I reached for Mom and she came over, wrapping her arms around both of us.

"I'm so excited," I whispered.

"I want to meet this boy you keep mentioning," Dad murmured.

I nodded. "Of course. Of course."

"Troy, right?" Mom asked.

I nodded. "Yeah. That's his name."

I released my parents and smiled at them as a wave of happiness rushed over me.

"I can't believe you guys are coming home for a bit with me," I said.

Dad cupped my cheeks. "We figured with everything you've been through, we could stand to be up there for a little while."

"How long?" I asked.

Mom shrugged. "I mean, we're retired. A few days. Couple weeks."

"Though, not long enough to get trapped in the first snow this year. We'll never get back here to the warm ocean waters if we stay that long," Dad said.

I kissed them both on their cheeks. "I love you guys so much."

Dad hugged me again. "We love you, too, princess."

We finished our breakfast and then I went upstairs to finish packing. I needed to send Troy a text message too. He needed to come with his car to get me from the airport. Not his bike.

Bike, bad.

Car, good.

Me: So, change of plans. I need you to drive your car to come get me. I'll explain later. I'll see you in a few hours!

I sent the message off and shoved my phone back into my purse. Then, I started to scan the hotel room. Trying to see if I had missed anything before we headed to the airport.

"This yours?!" Dad asked.

I looked over my shoulder and saw him holding up one of the hotel's blankets.

"Nope. That's for here," I said.

"What about this?" Mom asked.

I looked over and saw her holding up my phone charger.

"Oh, that is mine. Thank you," I said.

"You've got a sock over here," Dad said.

"You want to keep these miniature toiletries and everything?" Mom asked.

"She practically collects those things now."

"Well, I like donating them to shelters in our area."

I smiled at Mom. "Well, take them then. Donate them. They're as good as yours."

I zipped up my things before leaving my key cards behind in the room. Going to the airport with my parents felt so surreal. But, standing in line with them at TSA? I actually cried a little bit. Happy tears, of course. I was so glad they were coming home with me for a while. I had missed them. A lot. Ever since they moved so far away, I longed for them to be back home. To be closer to me so I could keep an eye on them. Or easily sneak away to snag one of my father's bear hugs or indulge in one of my mother's homemade meals.

"Honey, are you going to get that?"

Mom's voice snapped me from my mind. "What?"

"Your phone. It's buzzing," Dad said.

"Oh! Might be work. Hold on," I said.

But, when I took my phone out, I noticed Troy calling.

Uh-oh.

"Give me a second. I'll be right back," I said.

"You take your time. I'm going to go get us some snacks for the flight," Mom said.

"And I need some more coffee," Dad said.

I watched them walk away before I answered the phone. I leaned back in my chair, watching as our flight number flashed up on the screen. Twenty minutes until boarding. We had twenty minutes before we found our seats on the plane and made our way home.

Together.

As a family.

"Hey there," I said.

"I've been trying to call you all morning. Is everything okay?" he asked.

"Yeah. Did you get my message?"

"Yeah, that's why I'm calling. Why do we need my car? Is everything okay on your end?"

I snickered. "Well, uh..."

"Whatever it is, Sadie, let me help."

I smiled softly. "You're amazing, you know that?"

"Sadie, talk to me."

"My parents surprised me with coming back."

He paused. "What?"

I sighed. "I spent a lot of time with my parents while working down here this time. And they decided to surprise me by coming back for a few days. They're going to be on the flight with me. So, you won't just be picking me up."

I waited for him to get upset. Or for him to say no. Or for him to shoot me a million questions before finally sighing and getting frustrated that he had to meet my parents so early on in things.

That wasn't the reaction I got, though.

"Guess I should start cleaning the car, then. You guys gonna be hungry once you get off the plane?"

I paused. "You're not upset?"

He snickered. "No. I mean, I should shower. But I'm not upset. Why?"

I shrugged. "I don't know. Don't you think this is too early to be meeting parents and all that?"

"Do we really have a choice? Your parents want to come back with you. Probably to make sure you're okay. I'm not going to get mad at that. Ever step I've been taking lately has been to make sure you're okay."

"Wait, really?"

He chuckled. "Yes, really. You mean a lot to me. You're their daughter. Bring it on. Just tell me what they like to eat and drink, and I'll have it ready in case you guys need it."

I shook my head. "You're just outstanding."

"I know."

I giggled. "Yeah, yeah, yeah. Well, both of my parents are a fan of that smoothie place, Tropical Paradise."

"I don't blame them. It's a damn good place."

"She likes that all pineapple one and he's a chocolate peanut butter fan."

"What about you?"

I paused. "Do you think they still have that triple berry and banana one?"

"Don't tell me that's your favorite."

I groaned. "Oh, it's the best one on their menu."

"That one's my favorite too."

"Really? That's so funny."

"I'll make sure to have nice large ones for you guys once you arrive. Still a three forty-two arrival, right?"

I nodded. "Yep. Hasn't changed. Clear skies over here."

"Same here. I'll see you guys then."

"See you then, handsome."

I hung up the phone and slid it into my purse. And when I looked up, I saw my parents standing there. Grinning at me. Mom, with her bag of snacks, and Dad, with two cups of coffee. Smiling at me as if I had suddenly become pregnant with their first grandkid or some nonsense like that.

"What?" I asked.

"Handsome?" Mom asked.

"I take it you weren't talking about me," Dad said.

"You guys heard that?" I asked.

Mom nodded. "We were walking up when you said it."

"Didn't you hear us saying your name?" Dad asked.

"No, I didn't," I said.

He handed me one of the cups of coffee. "Well, then I really can't wait to meet the man who has distracted my daughter this way."

I shook my head, but the grin that slid across my face told the entire story. I felt like a kid in a candy shop, and I was anxious as to how this might go. The plane boarded and the flight home was smooth. Clear skies, despite the freezing cold temperatures as we approached Michigan. My parents always waited until everyone else was off the plane before they got off. A quirk of theirs I never did figure out. But, once we finally disembarked, we headed straight for baggage.

Where Troy already stood, waiting for us.

"Troy!" I exclaimed.

I tried not to seem too excited. But, his grin had me walking fast anyway. His grin brightened into a smile and my heart skipped a beat, watching as he made his way for me. My feet moved faster. He held his arms out for me. And as I threw my arms around his neck, he picked me up to swing me around.

Before my parents intervened.

"Whoa, ho, ho, ho. I think a father should shake a man's hand before he starts tossing my daughter around," Dad said.

"Oh my gosh, you're huge," Mom said.

"Mom." I hissed.

"Well, he is!" she squealed.

Troy chuckled. "It's nice to meet you, Mrs. Powers. And you, Mr. Powers."

I watched as Troy shook my father's hand. And Mom? Well, she went in for a hug like I figured she would. A hug that was a little too long, if I had anything to say about it. But Troy was a good sport about it. About everything, really. And when the hugs and handshakes had been exchanged, his hand fell to the middle of my back.

"So, how was the flight? Safe, I hope," Troy said.

"I like him already," Dad said.

"How nice of you to ask. It was very nice. Very safe," Mom said.

"Oh! I think that's our luggage," I said.

"No, no, no. I've got the luggage. Just point it out to me and I'll haul it. The three of you need free hands for the smoothies I've got waiting in the car," Troy said.

Mom gasped. "Please tell me he got them from—"

"He did," I said, smiling.

"Oh, he's perfect!" Mom exclaimed.

I fell apart in laughter before I looked up at Troy. Watching as he winked at me. All of this felt so ... right. So natural. So effortless. I didn't realize it could feel this way with a guy. Like, ever.

"Before I forget, Troy, thank you for taking such good care of our daughter," Dad said.

"Oh, yes. Thank you for that. We heard you let our daughter stay with you for a few days while this whole Luke debacle got sorted out," Mom said.

Troy heaved luggage off the conveyor belt. "It was nothing. My place is her place, so long as she needs it."

"Now *that's* the kind of man you need in your life, Sadie," Dad said.

"Especially with all the luggage he can haul at once," Mom said.

That comment made Troy bark with laughter, which caused all of us to laugh with one another again.

Making memories I hope we all continued to make as time went on.

Chapter 12

Troy

By the time I got everyone in the car, back to the house, and helped them unload their luggage, it was well past dinnertime. And I heard the grumbling of stomachs who weren't satiated by a mere smoothie. I looked around at their faces. At Sadie, glancing into the kitchen and looking more exhausted at the idea of cooking. At her father, who was practically rubbing his stomach in hunger. Despite the smoothie he chugged like a king. I even looked at her mother, who kept wiping at sweat on her brow and seemingly couldn't cool herself off long enough to enjoy the fact that she was home.

So, I came up with an idea to appease everyone.

"Who wants steak tonight?" I asked.

"Oh, I don't feel like cooking," Sadie said.

"I wasn't going to make you cook, beautiful."

Her mother sighed. "Aww, did you hear that?"

Her father grinned. "Yeah, I did."

I snickered. "Sadie, isn't there a steakhouse you reviewed a while back that's around here?"

She paused. "Well, not around this immediate area. But, we're probably only twenty minutes from it."

"Why don't we go there for dinner? I'm sure I could call and get a last-minute reservation. We could go, have a nice dinner, maybe some wine."

"You had me at steak," her dad said.

"And you've sunk me on wine," her mom said.

I laughed. "Sadie?"

She smiled. "I'll never turn down a good meal like that. Especially if it's with you."

"Awww!" her mother squealed.

"I just need to clean up a bit," her dad said.

"Oh, it's not that kind of a restaurant. If you just splash some water in your face, what you're wearing right now is fine," Sadie said.

"Khakis and a polo?" her dad asked.

She nodded. "Yep."

"What about what I'm wearing?" her mom asked.

I smiled. "I wouldn't change a thing about you, Mrs. Powers."

"Oh, and he lays it on thick. Good choice, Sadie. I'm proud of you," she said.

Sadie fell apart in giggles and the sound brought comfort to my heart.

"Well, splashing my face with water is still a good idea," her father said.

"Just let me brush my teeth really quickly," her mother said.

"I do need another shirt too. This one has a rip in the back," Sadie said.

"Well, then. Ten minutes. I'll go start the car and you guys can just come out when you're ready," I said.

I walked by and bent down to press a soft kiss to Sadie's forehead. Nothing long, and nothing salacious. But, enough for her to know I was glad to have her back home. She looked up at me with that cheeky little grin of hers, then cupped my cheek. Her thumb smoothed along my stubble. Her eyes twinkled with delight. I loved seeing her happy like this. Relaxed, without a care in the world to be given to anything else except what made her smile in the first place.

"See you out there soon," I murmured.

"Okay," she whispered.

She tapped my cheek softly, then I walked back out the front door. I cranked up the car and blasted the heat to keep things from frosting up already. A cold snap had descended over Michigan earlier than usual. It seemed fall only lasted a few days this year before the ice and the frost and the freezing temperatures took over. Nevertheless, that meant my favorite time of the year was upon us. Snow, and Christmas. Twinkling lights and roaring fireplaces. Even those cheesy Christmas movies I watched. Though, I'd never admit that to anyone.

Maybe Sadie will want to watch them with me.

"All right! Who's ready for some food?" Sadie asked.

She and her parents slipped quickly into the car before buckling their seat belts.

"I'm definitely ready for some food," I said.

"You look like you could eat three steaks in a sitting," her father said.

Sadie giggled. "I've seen him eat three entire dishes of food in one sitting."

"I mean, he's a growing boy! Look at him," her mother said.

"Yeah, I think you're doing plenty of that, Charlotte," her father said.

All of us laughed as I backed out of the driveway. Sadie definitely came with spitfire parents. It gave me a wonderful glimpse into how she'd become the woman she was today. And it was easy to figure out where she got everything from. Her sense of style from her mother. Her eyes, from her father. Her mother's nose. Her father's sassy sense of humor. Her mother's facial expressions.

She was the perfect amalgamation of the two of them.

And it was funny to watch.

"So, where do you guys live in Florida?" I asked.

"Near Fort Lauderdale," her mother said.

"That's a nice area. Did you guys always want to retire there?"

"We actually had our eyes set on Southern California for a spell. But we changed our minds after those nasty wildfires rolled through a few years back," her father said.

"And every year after that, practically," her mother said.

"We're much more equipped for hurricanes in Florida than we are for wildfires in California," he said.

"I don't blame you one bit for that one. Though, I'd like to not have to deal with any of that nonsense. Which is why Michigan is a nice compromise. No tornadoes. No moving ground. No hurricanes. No wildfires," I said.

"Yeah, just freezing cold winters that threaten frostbite within minutes, if it gets cold enough," her mother said.

I shrugged. "That's why I hibernate. I'm practically a bear of a man anyway."

Her father barked with laughter. "I like this one, Sadie. He's got nice jokes."

She snickered. "I'm glad you like them, Dad."

I peeked at her in the rearview mirror and I saw that look in her eye. That fire. That cheekiness. And I knew exactly what she was thinking.

He's got other nice things too.

"Bad girl," I mouthed.

And when she blushed, I knew I was spot on with my assessment.

Dinner was phenomenal, even with the massive crowd we had to contend with. It looked as if the restaurant was doing well. I mean, they even had Sadie's article framed and mounted on the wall! That was definitely a sight to see. Especially for her parents. They wanted to take a picture with their daughter in front of it, so I proudly snapped as many of them as they wanted. I knew it embarrassed Sadie, but I loved it. I loved seeing how much they cared for their daughter. How proud of her they were.

She came from a couple of good ones.

"So, what would you recommend on the menu?" her father asked.

"This filet mignon with the risotto sounds fantastic," her mother said.

"Oh, that was one of the dishes I got when I reviewed here. It's spectacular. You really should get it. And Dad, they *really* know how to throw down some perfect grill marks on their New York Strip," Sadie said.

"Sold!" he exclaimed.

I ordered a bottle of wine for the table and we indulged ourselves. The entire dinner was one big laugh after another. Stories of Sadie's childhood poured into stories of their childhood before they asked stories about my childhood. We got to know a great deal about one another, and the conversation never seemed to end. It was effortless, being around them. It warmed my heart, watching how they doted on Sadie. Listening to how proud they were of her and her concerted efforts to become the journalist she had always wanted to be. And the way she lit up around her parents was something I hadn't seen before. How relaxed she seemed.

I wanted to find a way to replicate that once they left.

"All right, where's the ticket?" her father asked.

"What ticket?" I asked.

"The bill, Troy," Sadie said softly.

"Oh, no. I already took care of it," I said.

"What?" her mother asked.

"You didn't. I was going to get dinner to thank you for helping us get to the house," he said.

I shrugged. "Well, too bad."

Her mother clapped her hands. "That is outstanding work. Usually, my husband never gives up the check to anyone."

"I'm getting the next dinner," he said.

"We'll see about that," I said, grinning.

I drove them all back to the house and walked them up to the door. And after they got inside, I pressed a soft kiss to Sadie's cheek.

"We'll catch up after your parents go home. Okay?" I murmured.

She nodded. "Okay."

"Have fun with them. Enjoy them while they're here."

She nuzzled her nose against my own. "I'll miss you."

I smiled. "I'll miss you too."

Then, with one more kiss to her cheek, I made my way back to my car.

On the way home, I called my mother. Seeing Sadie with her parents reinforced just how much I cared for my own mother. Granted, I didn't have two parents in the picture. But that didn't mean shit. Mom had played the role of two parents my entire life. And I had a sudden aching feeling in the pit of my stomach to see her. Or, at least hear her voice.

"Hey there, sweetheart. Can you make it quick? In the middle of a class."

She huffed and puffed as music thudded on the other side of the phone.

"Just calling to tell you that I love you," I said.

She giggled. "Love you, too, sweetheart. I'll call you after class. Okay?"

"If you can. If you pass out before then because you're old, I understand that too."

"I hate you."

I smiled. "Never."

She giggled. "Did Sadie get home okay?"

"You have a class, Mom."

"Just the one question."

I nodded. "She did get home okay."

"Good. That's good. I'm glad she's got someone like you. Listen, I gotta go. But, breakfast in the morning? Yeah?"

I smiled. "Sounds good. I'll pick you up around six thirty?"

"Perfect. See you then. Love you."

"I love you too."

The rest of my evening was spent relaxing and wondering what Sadie and her parents were up to. And when morning came around, she was the first thing on my mind. My alarm blared from my phone, signaling the fact that I had to get my ass out of bed. I needed to pick Mom up for breakfast, and I also needed to get myself a decent shower.

But not before I messaged Sadie.

Me: Thinking about you. I hope you and your parents have a great day today.

"Now, shower time." I grunted.

The shower was quick. Quicker than I wanted it to be, really. But that meant more time with Mom that morning. I got dressed and headed to her place, ready to pick her up. However, I didn't see her car in its usual parking space.

And before I could call her on my cell phone, it dinged with a text.

Mom: Get to work. Now.

She sure as hell didn't have to tell me twice either.

I backed out and raced across town. Why Mom lived so far away from the gym, I'd never understand. But urgency bled through my veins. The text message didn't bode well for anyone. And I wondered what kind of hellfire I was about to walk into. I skidded around corners and rushed down back alley streets. Doing anything I could to shave off time and get to work quicker. The gym didn't open for another hour and a half. What in the world could have possibly happened that required people to be there an hour and a half early?

However, when I pulled into the parking lot, I noticed Mom wasn't the only person there. I also saw Paris. With her arm around Wren and their faces full of smiles.

What the fuck is going on?

I pulled into a parking space and threw my door open. Holy fucking hell, it was only eleven degrees outside. How the hell were they standing out here like this? I shivered as I closed my car door. I walked over to them in the middle of the parking lot where Mom couldn't stop hugging Paris. They jumped up and down as Wren laughed. Adding to my confused state.

"Someone want to fill me in on what the fuck's happening?" I asked.

"They picked us," Wren said.

I blinked. "Who?"

"Are you kidding me? The account, Troy!" Mom exclaimed.

She almost knocked me over with a hug. But I still didn't understand what they were talking about.

"I don't get it. What account?" I asked.

"The advertising account? That thing we applied for a few months back?" Paris asked.

"The thing my brother's advertising group is doing," Wren said.

Holy shit. I'd forgotten all about that.

"Wait a second. They picked us for that?" I asked.

"Yes!" Mom exclaimed.

"Holy shit! They picked us!" I yelled.

"You guys are going to be the new face of the small business section of Detroit Marketing Services," Wren said, smiling.

I wrapped my mother and Paris up in a massive hug. We jumped around in the parking lot before Wren got in on the action. I couldn't believe it. I knew that shit was a longshot to begin with. But, after not hearing anything for over two months, I figured we had gotten rejected.

"Holy shit, this is amazing," I said.

I let go of everyone before running my hands through my hair.

"There's so much we have to do. We have to kick our rebranding into gear. Paris, have you ordered those new cards of ours yet?" Mom asked.

"Put in the order two days ago. They should arrive tomorrow," she said.

"Sweetheart, you changed out all the flyers and logos we had across town, right?" Mom asked.

I nodded. "Got a few more to do today, but everything else—including online—has been changed."

"The website still needs to be updated, though. It's still got a bit of purple on it," Paris said.

"I want that to be a top priority today. We need the rebranding to go out with this new phase of marketing we've been picked for. I don't want any stone unturned," Mom said.

"But first? A celebratory breakfast. My treat," Wren said.

"And drinks tonight. Call everyone!" I said.

Mom pointed at me. "Great idea. I'll send out a mass text."

"And don't forget to ask Sadie," Paris said.

The grin on her face made me chuckle.

"I'll extend an invitation. But her parents are in town. Not sure if that'll be something they all want to do. I'll definitely invite them, though," I said.

"Wait, her parents are in town? Since when?" Mom asked.

I paused. "Since yesterday."

"You mean, when you picked her up from the airport."

I nodded. "Yep."

Her jaw dropped open. "You met her parents and you didn't even tell me?!"

Paris blinked. "You met Sadie's parents already?"

Wren chuckled. "What are they like?"

I rolled my eyes. "One thing at a time. Invitations, breakfast, work-day, then we can tackle all this shit over drinks tonight."

"You mean, you're going to make your poor old mother wait for answers to these pertinent questions?" Mom asked.

I shrugged. "You called yourself 'old' that time. Not me."

She paused. "When the hell have you ever called me old?"

Wren chuckled. "Uh-oh."

Paris snickered. "You stepped in it this time."

"Breakfast and invitations! Go!" I exclaimed.

Then, I quickly slipped back into my car. Ready to get some damn food in my stomach before I passed out from hunger.

Or worse. Kept getting poked and prodded by my loving, old, nosey-ass mother.

Chapter 13

Sadie

"You sure you guys are up for something like this?" I asked.

"What? You think we can't handle a few drinks out? What do you think we've been doing during our retirement?" Mom asked.

"You're the one who fell asleep at that concert, by the way," Dad said.

"The music was too soothing! I thought there was going to be some oomph to it," I said.

"Well, at any rate, we'll be just fine. I'm just excited to meet some more of your friends. Is Uma joining us?" Mom asked.

"Yeah, we haven't gotten a chance to see her yet," Dad said.

"No, she can't get off work. She's working a double because someone called in sick. She won't be in until late, and even then, she'll crash immediately. You guys might see her when she gets up in the morning, though," I said.

"And speaking of work, do you go back in tomorrow?" Mom asked.

"Because if you do, you might not want to—"

I held up my hand, interrupting Dad. "I do work tomorrow, but I can also work from home. I've already messaged my editor. He knows you guys are in town with me. He's given me leeway these past few weeks to work from home, if necessary. Plus, he'll be fine for a couple of days, at least. He's got the articles he needs from me to run next week. So, if I work from home? It won't be much anyway," I said.

Dad cupped my cheek. "I'm so proud of you, princess."

I smiled. "Thanks, Daddy."

"Well, if the two of you emotional mush balls are ready, I want myself a margarita," Mom said.

My eyebrows rose. "Since when do you drink margaritas?"

"I've always had them. I just never indulged in them until you went to sleep as a child," she said.

"Yeah, your mother's and my 'fun times' never happened until you were—"

I held up my hand again. "Okay, yikes. That's enough."

My parents laughed as I searched around for my things.

"All right. I'm ready whenever you guys are," I said.

"Lead the way, honey," Mom said.

"Will they have coffee at this bar, you think?" Dad asked.

Mom rolled her eyes. "I swear, he chugs more of the stuff now than he did when he was working those backward shifts at the cable company."

"Coffee keeps me alive." Dad hissed playfully.

I giggled. "You guys are too much. Come on. We're going to be late."

The drive back into Detroit seemed a bit shorter than usual. And when we pulled into the parking lot for the bar, flurries of snow began falling. I stepped out of the car and closed my eyes. I felt the snowflakes tumbling against my skin. Melting, and cooling, and covering me in the beginning stages of one of the most fantastic times of the year.

"Will you guys make it back for Christmas?" I asked.

I opened my eyes and found my parents smiling at me.

"We wouldn't miss that holiday with you for the world," Dad said.

Then, he pulled me in and kissed me against my forehead.

"Now, it's margarita time. Woo-hoo!" Mom exclaimed.

I groaned. "Oh, this was a bad idea."

Dad wrapped his arm around me. "Let her have some fun. We both worked hard during our early years. Retirement is when we get to enjoy not having to abide by so many rules. You'll understand once you get there."

I leaned my head against his shoulder. "Yeah, maybe so."

We walked into the bar and Troy waved us down. The smell of cheese fries and wings pulled me to the table. But the glass of wine Troy had sitting out for me made me smile. I slid into the booth, nestling tightly against him. And as introductions were made, it almost seemed as if we all had known one another for ages.

Especially with how Troy's mother got to talking with my parents.

"Did you see the snow outside?" I asked.

I looked up at Troy and found him grinning down at me.

"It's coming down harder now. We might actually have a small coating before we all go to leave tonight."

I smiled. "I love this time of the year. The snow. The holidays. The lights."

"The movies."

"What?"

He furrowed his brow. "What?"

"You said 'the movies.' What movies?"

He paused. "You know, just those Christmas movies."

"You mean, like, *The Grinch*? Or, like, the Hallmark movies?"

"Both?"

I sat up. "You like the Hallmark Christmas movies?"

"Shh, can you keep that down a bit?"

"Everyone's talking around us. It's fine."

"Is that so?" Wren asked.

My eyes darted around and I found everyone staring at us. They all had cheeky smiles on their faces, and I heard Troy let out a soft groan. Paris leaned over the table and tapped him on the forearm. Making him sigh before he cast her a sharp glare.

"What?" Troy asked.

"Does the big, bad biker boy like his Christmas movies?" she asked.

Wren snickered. "I didn't know you were a fan of sappy love story Christmas movies."

"Oh, I love those things. I really shouldn't, but I do. They all have the same plot," his mother said.

"Right?" my mother asked. "I mean, they hate each other in the beginning, and halfway through the movie they're kissing!"

"It's her favorite part," my father said.

"Uh-oh," I said flatly.

I looked up at Troy and found him shaking his head.

"Sorry," I whispered.

He held me tightly. "You can repay me by watching a few of those sappy movies with me."

I grinned. "Deal."

"All right. I'd like to make a toast really quickly," Wren said.

He stood from his seat and picked up his beer as we all turned to face him.

"To Paris and Troy. I know you guys accuse me of putting in a good word with my brother. But, I can assure you, this was your hard work alone that got you this marketing account. It's an honor to be here celebrating with you guys. Watching you pull all this off when I remember how nervous you guys were in the beginning to open this gym. Congratulations. You guys deserve this."

"That's so sweet," my mother whispered.

"He's long-winded, he's not done yet," Troy's mother whispered back.

Wren drew in a deep breath. "And another thing. I want to especially toast Paris. Because without her, some things in my life wouldn't be possible right now. Like the happiness I feel inside. Or how nice my apartment looks now. Or how my loneliness has been chased away because of her smile. And her embrace. You're the best thing that's ever happened to me. To this gym. To all of our lives. Not only is this a toast for the future of the gym. But, it's a toast to our future, and whatever it might bring."

"Oh, Wren," Paris said.

"That's so sweet," Mom squealed.

"I have love for you, Paris. I don't know if I can physically say that statement yet. But, it's there. Every time I look at you. Every time you smile at me. My heart physically leaps. Thank you for putting up with my bullshit. And thank you for accepting me as, well, me," Wren said.

"I have love for you, too, Wren," Paris said breathlessly.

"To the gym!" Wren exclaimed.

We all held up our glasses. "To the gym!"

"And to the woman quickly becoming the light of my life," Wren said.

Then, we all finally clinked glasses before he sat back down.

The celebration didn't last nearly as long as anyone wanted it to. Mostly because everyone had to get up for work in the morning. But, also because of the snow. It came down harder. Faster. In buckets, almost. And while it was beautiful, it also stuck to the roads. Still, we were able to enjoy some food and some drinks before the snow finally pushed us out. Troy was right. Some of it was already sticking to the roads. And I didn't want to take the chance that it might start building up before we could get out of there.

Dad still tried to wrestle the bill away from Troy. But, he was easily able to convince my father that this was a business outing, so it needed to go on the business card. Which my father seemed okay with, since it wasn't technically Troy paying at all. We tossed our drinks back before getting up. Then, we braced for the ever-blessed cold as the pouring snow plummeted the temperature around us.

"I'll text you in the morning," Troy said.

And after pressing his lips against mine for a kiss, a round of cheers echoed from the cars around us. My parents, whooping and hollering from inside the car. Paris and Wren, cheering from the back of his bike.

Troy's mother, beating on the steering wheel of her truck. It made me blush. But, it didn't stop Troy from going in for another kiss. And then another. Until he had me bent back, with his arms holding me close.

"Mmm, cheese fries taste good on you," he murmured.

I giggled. "You're a mess. Help me up."

"What if I like you this way?"

"You might not want my father hearing something like that come from you."

He paused. "Good point."

He helped me upright before opening my car door for me. He even offered me his hand, which made my mother practically sigh with content. He winked at me as I buckled myself in. Even going so far as to shut my car door for me.

"Such a gentleman," Mom swooned.

"She's had one too many margaritas, I think," I said, giggling.

"She's right, though. He seems like a good man," Dad said.

And as I watched Troy venture back to his own bike, I nodded.

"Yeah. He is a good man," I said.

It had been a good night. A very, very good night. And I was so glad my parents were here to witness it. To partake in it. To be part of the memory. Wren honked the horn on his bike before him and Paris made their leave. Troy's mother did the same, honking the horn of her truck before waving at us. Then, Troy pulled out, motioning for me to get behind him.

"What's he doing?" Mom asked.

I snickered. "He's wanting me to follow him."

"Why's that?"

I sighed. "So he can make sure we get to the outer city limits safely."

Mom put her hand on my shoulder. "Don't let go of this one, sweetheart."

I smiled. "Trust me, I don't intend to."

Then, I backed out of the parking space, pulled up behind Troy, and followed his every turn. Until he guided us out of town on the safest roads. During a flash snow pileup. Before he turned around to head back to his own place.

"He's waving. He's waving. Wave at him, guys!" Dad said cheerfully.

And when I waved at Troy, he blew me a kiss.

Before speeding off into the snow while I drove the rest of us back home.

Chapter 14

Troy

I sprayed the weights down and wiped them while silently cursing to myself. Now that we had this new advertising account, I noticed every single little thing that needed to be fixed in the gym. Like, the small stains appearing on the ceiling, seemingly from out of nowhere. I already had a plumber in here twice this week to see if any of the pipes were leaking. I had roofers on top of the damn place now to figure out if any sort of water damage was causing the issue before I simply painted over it to try and make it a uniform color again. If shit was broken, I wanted it fixed. Because in one month's time, our entire gym would be the new face of this small business advertisement push.

Which meant we'd be on billboards. And in commercials. And on ads online.

Why the fuck won't people just clean these damn weights?

"Paris!"

"Yeah!?"

"Send out an email reminder to our gym users about cleaning the damn equipment!"

She poked her head around the corner. "What's going on?"

I stood up. "The damn weights are starting to get streaked with all sorts of shit because people aren't cleaning up after themselves. I want to start inducing some sort of a penalty against their accounts or something if we catch them not cleaning down equipment they sweat and spit on for hours at a time during the week."

"That might not be the best thing to do before this marketing push."

I groaned. "Then, just send out the email reminder. But, we have to start doing something. The weights look terrible, and a few of the machines have the beginning stages of rust on them because of sweat drying and lingering and not being wiped up."

"You know we've got that Rust-O-Gone stuff in the—?"

I held up the bottle. "Yep. Already getting to work on it."

"Troy!"

I whipped my head around. "Wren?"

"Troy! Troy! Where the hell are you?"

The panic in his voice sent me running. I heard Paris hot on my heels, but I quickly left her in my dust. I dropped everything from my hands and tore down the hallway, quickly dodging people as I ran for Wren's voice.

"Troy!" he roared.

I came around the corner and ran straight into him. Knocking him down on the ground. He looked positively frantic. I helped him to his feet as his eyes grew wider and wider. And as soon as he opened his mouth, I already knew what he was going to say.

"It's Luke, isn't it?" I asked.

He panted. "My buddy at the station just called me. I hadn't even gotten into work when I—"

I cupped his face. "Tell me what happened."

"Luke lost his detail. He was being moved from county jail to the courthouse with his lawyer. And Luke just slipped away."

Paris scoffed. "How the fuck is that even possible?"

My hands fell to his shoulders. "Do you know anything else? Anything at all?"

Wren shook his head. "I whipped a U-turn in the middle of the road the second I got the call. I kept calling your cell. Why the fuck didn't you pick up?"

"He's been cleaning all morning. He's paranoid about this advertising thing," Paris said.

"I need to call Sadie," I said.

I brushed passed Wren and sprinted for my office. My legs carried me as quickly as I could go. I heard people cursing my name as I charged by. I heard my mother yelling at me. Telling me to slow my roll. To watch where I was going. But if she knew what was happening right now? She'd be telling me to pick up the fucking pace.

I slammed into my office, almost taking the door off the damn hinges before I reached for my phone.

I dialed Sadie's number and held the phone to my ear.

"Come on, come on. Pick up," I murmured.

But all it did was ring. It rang and it rang. And it rang some more. I hung up and tried again. I propped my phone against my shoulder and gathered up my things as footsteps came rumbling down the hallway. Footsteps I recognized.

"Wren, how long ago did this happen?" I asked.

"I'll never understand how you do that," he said breathlessly.

"Just answer the damn question," I said.

"Hello, this is Sadie Powers with the Detroit Metro—"

"Shit!" I exclaimed.

I hung up the phone and tried yet again as I stared at Wren.

"Well?" I asked.

"Uh, it—I got the call ten or so minutes ago. And before that, Luke had been out of custody many fifteen, twenty minutes?" he asked.

"And the courthouse is where?"

"Ten minutes east of here."

I paused. "You mean, the Washington side of the city. Where Sadie lives."

"Hello, this is Sadie Powers with Detroi—"

"Fuck." I hissed.

I hung up the phone when her voicemail message rolled through my ear again. I shoved my phone into my pocket and brushed passed Wren. I knocked shoulders with Paris as I headed for my mother's office. But she was already standing at her doorway by the time I got there.

"Mom, I have to head out and—"

She grabbed my shoulders and kissed my cheek.

"Go get her. And call me the second you have her. Okay?" she asked.

I hugged her close. "Thanks, Mom."

The rest of the time was a blur. I cranked up my car and sped all the way to Sadie's place. On the one hand, I didn't want to think Luke was stupid enough to approach the house while her parents were there. On the other hand, though, I didn't think he was stupid enough to come after me. And he did. Which meant I had to assume he didn't have an issue with attacking folks like Sadie's parents.

"Piece of trash little fucker." I growled.

I honked my horn and swerved around traffic. It wasn't until I saw Wren's lights in my rearview mirror that I noticed why someone hadn't already pulled me over. He sped up to my window and I saw Paris in the front seat of his cruiser. Guess Mom was on her own this morning for work. Wren pointed to the exit for Sadie's house before cutting in front of me. Leading the cavalry and making sure none of the other officers we were blazing by pulled us over.

Then, my cell phone rang.

"Sadie? I'm on my way to your house. Lock all the doors. Luke's—"

"Dude, it's me. It's me," Wren said.

I furrowed my brow. "The fuck you calling me for?"

"Should we call Uma?" he asked.

I blinked. "Why? What's going on in your mind?"

I heard some wrestling on the other end of the line before Paris's voice hit my ears.

"It's a bit farfetched that he's already gotten out here to Sadie. But, do you think the man's crazy enough to go after Uma? I mean, he went after you. Shouldn't we at least warn Uma what's going on in case Luke gets some wild hair up his ass to hurt her or something? You know, to get back at Sadie?"

"Get back at her for what? She didn't do anything!" I exclaimed.

"I know that, Troy. We all know that. But, Luke doesn't know that. You gotta think like him for a second."

I sighed. "She should know what's going on, anyway. She lives at the damn house. She's best friends with Sadie. Do you have her number?"

"I do. I'll give her a call now," she said.

"Thanks."

I hung up the phone as we barreled into Sadie's neighborhood. This would, no doubt, cause her parents to lengthen their visit. Which meant more sitting ducks in that house. The more this shit got out of hand, the more I wanted to convince myself that staying over at Sadie's place was a good idea. I mean, I couldn't fit all those people in my con-do. But, they had room for one more person. Right?

I could provide my own bed. Make meals. Drive Sadie into work. Wren could station patrol cars outside of the house for her parents.

The list went on inside my brain as we pulled into the driveway.

I slammed out of the car, thankful to see Sadie's still in the drive-way. Holy shit, in my franticness, it didn't even occur to me that she might've just gone into the office. I cursed myself. I had to keep my head screwed on straight. I rushed up to the front door with Wren and Paris, my fist knocking heavily against the door.

"Sadie! Open up! It's Troy!" I roared.

But, when her father swung the door open, looking completely un-bothered, I didn't know whether to be relieved or more concerned.

"Everything okay? You sound upset," he said.

"Where's Sadie? I have to talk with her," I said.

"She's in the kitchen with her mother. They've been cooking up a storm all morning. You guys want to come in? I'm sure there's plenty of food for everyone," he said.

I slipped past him. "Sadie!"

"Troy?" she asked.

I stormed into the kitchen and found her elbow-deep in what looked like a massive chicken.

"Sadie, why aren't you picking up your phone?" I asked.

She snickered. "Well, if you can't tell, I'm in the process of fondling a chicken."

"Sadie." Her mother hissed.

"Get your arm out of that chicken and listen to us," Paris said.

Sadie furrowed her brow. "Why do you guys look like you've just seen a ghost?"

And when Wren stepped forward, I watched tears rush her eyes.

"Oh no," she said.

"What is it?" her mother asked.

"What's all this commotion about?" her father asked.

"Sadie, look at me. I promise, you're safe," I said.

"What happened? Where is he?" she asked.

"Where's who?" her mother asked.

"What?" her father asked.

I held up my hand, commanding complete silence. Then, I walked over to Sadie and cupped the back of her head with my hand.

"I need you to look into my eyes, okay?" I asked.

She nodded softly. "Okay."

"Luke was being transferred to the courthouse today for his first court hearing. He somehow lost his detail," I said.

"What?" she asked breathlessly.

"How is that even possible?" her father asked.

Wren piped up. "My officers are doing all they can to track him down. He couldn't have gotten far. It's all hands on deck throughout the city until he's found. But, do you know of anyone in his life who might be able to take him in? Someone in the city? Or someone who might've helped him escape?"

Sadie shook her head quickly. "Uh, no. No, I don't. I never, um, he doesn't have family, to my knowledge. Not anywhere around here."

"What about friends?" I asked.

She shook her head. "No. He always told me he was a homebody. Too introverted to make friends."

"What does this mean for our daughter?" her father asked.

"What can we do?" her mother asked.

"What else do you know?" Sadie whispered.

I shook my head. "Not much. Wren?"

He shrugged. "I'll update you guys as I know. But, what I do know is that he slipped his detail while being transferred with his lawyer to the courthouse. It was swift, so some of my guys think it might have been planned. But, even if it was, we don't know how he did it. He wasn't allowed phone calls or visitors."

"Does that mean he's friends with someone on the inside?" Sadie asked.

The entire room fell silent as we all looked to Wren for answers.

"While I don't like to usually entertain the idea that one of our own is corrupt, it's plausible," he said.

"Don't leave any stone unturned. You know what this man's capable of when he's acting like an idiot," I said.

"I need to go get my phone. I'm sure the station will call me at any second," Sadie said breathlessly.

"Come on, I'll go with you," Paris said.

I was reluctant to relinquish her. But, I did all the same. Sadie washed herself off at the kitchen sink before backtracking with Paris. And already, I heard her sniffling. The sound broke my heart. I closed my eyes and sank against the kitchen island. Wren clapped my shoulder, trying to massage the tension out of my body. It was no use, though.

I was officially back on my toes.

"Thank you," her father said.

I slowly opened my eyes. "What?"

"For coming out all this way the second you heard. It shows me how much you care about Sadie," he said.

"He's right. You're clearly worried about her. She needs more of that in her life," her mother said.

I shrugged. "I care about your daughter. I've seen what this man can do to her."

Her father swallowed hard. "We raised Sadie to be strong. But, we worry that maybe she's too strong at times."

"As in, she doesn't know when to ask for help," her mother said.

"Well, she doesn't have to ask with me. She gets it, whether she likes it or not," I said.

He snickered. "She might not like to hear that, but it brings me comfort to know she's got friends like you."

"And you too. Wren, right?" she asked.

Wren nodded. "Yes, ma'am. It's nice to see you again. I just hate that it's under these circumstances."

"Yes. Uh-huh. Do you know anything else?" Sadie asked.

Her voice hit my ears and I whipped around. Paris led her back into the kitchen, and I saw her already on the phone. Paris rubbed her back as Sadie wiped at her tears. She went to stand by her father's side and I resisted the urge to pull her toward me. I understood that feeling. Sometimes, a girl just needed her father. Like I just needed my mother sometimes.

"Okay. Yes. Thank you. I'll keep my phone with me. Uh-huh. Thank you. Bye," she said.

"So?" I asked.

She sighed as she set her phone down on the kitchen counter.

"All they know right now is that the lawyer wasn't in on anything. She's claiming she didn't help in any way, and they're inclined to believe her because, apparently, Luke knocked her out," she said.

"What? They didn't tell me that part," Wren said.

"They haven't seen him, but they're combing the city. Blocking off alleyways and such. Establishing checkpoints at all the major exits and entrances into the city. But, it's all they can do right now," she said.

I felt my blood boiling. I had to keep my focus on Sadie, though. Not my own whims and wishes to literally tear this man limb from limb the next time I saw him.

"What can we do for you?" I asked.

And as Sadie's eyes found mine, the rest of the world faded away.

As the entirety of my focus settled onto her.

Chapter 15

Sadie

I looked into the eyes of those surrounding me, and I saw panic. Worry. Frustration. Uneasiness. Yet, I felt none of those things. It was almost like an out-of-body experience. Like I wasn't really experiencing what they were. I mean, I heard them. Luke was gone again. In the wind. Running around the city, to who knew what. And yet, I didn't feel the same panic and the same worry and the same uneasiness that filtered around me.

I just ... was.

"We should get your security guy here to see if he can push me up in the queue. Even if we need to pay him the full installation fee. Having that system now rather than later is going to help give everyone peace of mind," I said.

"I can do that. I'll call Duke now," Troy said.

"What else do you need?" Wren asked.

"Patrols in the neighborhood would be nice. You know, a more metered presence in the area. And maybe around where I work," I said.

"You could work from home, honey. That's an option, right?" Mom asked.

"Which is why the patrols should happen in both places, yes," I said.

"I'll put in the call now," Wren said.

"Is there anything else you need?" Paris asked.

I sighed. "No. Not really. I mean, it's just a waiting game at this point. Unless you guys want to form a search party and go find Luke ourselves. The only thing I really can do is stay safe, use my training if I need to, and keep an eye out."

"Your training? What training?" Dad asked.

"Remember those kickboxing and self-defense classes I mentioned a few days ago?" I asked.

"I don't think you mentioned self-defense," Mom said.

"Well, that's my fault, then. But, yes. I'm taking self-defense, and Troy teaches that class as well. Along with Wren. I take it with Paris, Uma, and a few other people twice a week," I said.

Dad set his hand on my shoulder. "I'm so sorry you've been dealing with this without us."

"We should stay longer, Frank. She needs our support right now," Mom said.

"You guys don't have to do that if you don't want to. Snow's pushing in quicker. You guys are going to get stuck," I said.

"We'd rather be here with you, helping to keep you safe, than worrying about you day and night from Florida," Dad said.

"We can talk about it. How's that sound?" I asked.

"All right, I just got off the phone with Duke. I got the house bumped all the way up to this afternoon. He should be here with an install crew around two, and they won't leave until you're completely set up and connected," Troy said.

I smiled. "Perfect."

Wren walked back into the kitchen. "I just upped the patrols around your office as well as Uma's hospital. The department is in the process of communicating with the one here to up the patrols over on this end too."

"There has to be something more we can do, though," Paris said.

"Yeah, don't hesitate to ask. Now's not the time to get stingy," Dad said.

I shrugged. "I know you guys don't want to hear it, but that's all we can do right now. Get the alarm system in the house, get patrols up, and stay vigilant until Luke is back in custody."

"You're right. I don't like that at all," Mom said.

"Isn't there something we can do, baby?" Paris asked Wren.

I looked over at Troy and saw a mixture of anger and exhaustion in his face. I felt terrible for it too. Had I not come into his life, he wouldn't have to be dealing with this shit. Constantly running around behind me. Helping me to clean up my terrible mistakes.

"Honey, did you hear the man?" Mom asked.

I felt her shake my shoulder. "What?"

"Wren. He asked how you are on groceries," Dad said.

"I'm just trying to prevent how much you need to go outside. You know, if you don't have to," Wren said.

I snickered. "I don't have to contain myself to a house. If anything, that makes me a sitting duck. Luke doesn't get to rip my life away just because he got away somehow."

"But that doesn't mean you have to be put in the public eye all the time. Especially when we don't know where he is," Mom said.

I sighed. "I know you guys are worried. I get it. But I can make grocery runs, if necessary. I can go to my office. I can work, guys. I don't need to be quarantined to a house."

"We're not trying to do anything like that. We're just—"

I interrupted Troy's argument. "Then, stop acting like it. We're doing what we can, and that's all we can do."

I pulled away from everyone and slipped into the living room. The kitchen seemed crowded, and I didn't want to be there any longer. I walked over to the window. One that looked out toward the backyard. I gazed upon the snow-covered ground. The small, personal horizon that severed the smooth backyard snow away from the line of trees that signified the beginning of the woods. The wooded areas of Washington were gorgeous year-round. Babbling brooks and hiking trails. In the summers, they came alive with animals and flowers and the sound of crickets at night. And during winter, everything looked as if it were coated in a thin sheet of delicate glass.

What is happening to my life?

"Princess?"

I felt my father's hand slip into mine as he stood beside me.

"Hey, Daddy."

He licked his lips. "You don't want us here, do you?"

I snickered. "It isn't that I don't want you here. But, I feel this need to protect you guys."

"We feel that same need to protect you too."

I turned toward him. "You guys don't get it, though. Luke went after Troy. He hit his female lawyer to get away. If he comes at me, in any way, I don't want you and Mom caught in the crosshairs of that."

"We love you, and we aren't going anywhere."

"What if I told you that you could do more help from Florida than you ever could from here?"

Mom came up behind me. "I'd ask you why that is, because all we want to do is help."

I took my mother's hand in my free one as we all stood by the window.

"If I'm worried constantly about you two, and how you're doing, and what you're up to, and whether or not you're safe, I can't think clearly for myself. I won't be paying attention while I'm out and about. While I'm grocery shopping. Or working. Or with Troy. I won't be able to think about anything else, and that includes defending myself should something happen. You can ask Troy. Or Paris. Or Uma. Or anyone else. The number one rule in my self-defense class is—"

"To always be focused," Mom said.

I blinked. "Yeah. How do you know that?"

She grinned. "You're not the only one who knows how to defend herself in this family, sweetheart."

I snickered. "Is something happening down in Florida I should know about?"

"Not at all. But, I understand where you're coming from, despite the fact that I'm worried. Taking those classes helps me to feel more secure when I'm walking around Fort Lauderdale without your father. And I'm always focused. Always in tune with my surroundings. Always keeping an eye trained toward my back."

I smiled. "Sounds like they're teaching you well."

She sighed. "We don't want to leave you here."

Dad butted in. "But, we will, if you really want it."

I nodded. "We have this. There's nothing more that can be done than what's already being done currently. Putting more bodies here just creates more tension, more stress, and more people to protect."

"So, I guess there's no convincing you to come to Florida until this is all settled, huh?" Dad asked.

I giggled. "No. Definitely not."

"You've always been a cold-weather person," Mom said.

"And you two were made for the south," I said.

Dad sighed heavily before I drew them both in for a hug. I knew they weren't happy with it. I knew they weren't happy with the decisions I had made. But I knew I was right.

And somewhere, deep down, they knew it, too.

"Our flight leaves tomorrow at nine fourteen in the morning," Dad said.

"So, we'll need to be back at the airport no later than seven in the morning," Mom said.

I pushed them both out, nodding. "We can make that happen. Definitely."

"And I'll be driving, just so you know. No arguing either. I'll be here by six thirty or so," Troy said.

Dad thumbed over his shoulder. "I like him."

Mom smiled. "Me too. You've found a good one in him."

I looked over at Troy and smiled before he moseyed back around the corner. Disappearing into the kitchen.

"Yeah, I have," I said.

Paris called out, "So, I don't know if anyone else is feeling it. But, I'm starving."

Mom pointed behind her. "And I like her. She's got an appetite like me. Paris! Yeah! I'm hungry too!"

"Mind if the boys start—I mean—finish cooking, then?" Paris asked.

I paused. "What?"

My parents and I made our way back into the kitchen, only to find Wren and Troy creating a storm in my kitchen. There was bacon already sitting on the stove and Wren had the chicken basted and ready to stick in the oven. Paris held her hands up and slowly backed away. As if Wren had threatened her life with the barrel of the gun on his hip if she didn't get out of his way. I giggled at the sight. How meticulous the guys were. How focused they were in their concerted cooking efforts. And mere seconds later, the smell of coffee filled the kitchen.

"Now, we're talkin," Dad said.

"Get me a mug too. We can take it into the living room and put on a nice movie," Mom said.

"It's the perfect snowy morning for a Christmas movie, don't you think?" Paris asked.

Troy peeked over his shoulder and grinned at me. Making my heart seize in my chest.

"Yeah, I think it is," I said.

"I vote a Hallmark movie. Just for Troy," Wren said, chuckling.

"Actually, that doesn't sound like a bad idea," I said.

"A woman after my own heart," Troy said.

I felt my parents smiling brightly at me as my cheeks flushed.

"All right, who wants creamer and sugar for their coffee. Because that's the last I'm letting you guys trollop around in this kitchen until we're done cooking," Wren said.

I paused. "Did you just say 'trollop'?"

Paris handed me a mug of coffee. "Trust me, you haven't seen the full kaleidoscope of Wren and his mood swings until you've tried to mess with him while he's cooking. And we've had enough excitement for the morning."

"I'll take the cream and sugar into the room with us," Dad said.

"I've got the pot of coffee!" Mom exclaimed.

"Just, like, the whole pot? Leave me some, at least!" Troy yelled.

And despite the hell that had fallen back into my lap, things somehow felt relaxed again. Normal. Beautiful, and ... and good.

At least Luke couldn't take that away from us.

The bond we all apparently shared.

Chapter 16

Troy

I was thankful for the amazing amount of food there was in the house to cook. Because Wren and I went on a spree. It was how I blew off steam, and I knew it was helping to get his mind off shit too. I didn't like this. None of us liked this scenario. But, between the food, the movies, and the company? Things were bearable.

Until Duke got to the house.

"Someone order one top-of-the-line security system?" he asked coyly.

It ripped me out of dreamland and landed me back in reality.

"Hey there. Thanks for this. Come on in. Wren and I are here to help you too," I said.

"Oh, you guys don't need to do that if you don't want to. I'm sure you have other places to be," Sadie said.

"Better places than staying here and making sure you're all right? Over my dead body," I said.

"Come here, I'll show you where we want sensors installed," Wren said.

"Shouldn't I be the one to do that?" Sadie asked.

I furrowed my brow. I heard the tension growing in her voice, but I didn't know why.

"Just let him help. He likes feeling useful," I said.

But Sadie intercepted Duke anyway. "Hi, I'm Sadie. This is actually my house, believe it or not. And I'm more than capable of showing you where I want everything. Come with me."

Duke looked back at me and I shrugged. I saw shock and confusion on her parents' faces at the random outburst. Especially since Sadie had been laughing at a movie only seconds ago. I tried to brush it off, though. Sadie walked him around the house, showing him all the points of vulnerability, while Wren and I cleaned things up. Did the dishes. Put away leftovers and generally wiped the kitchen down.

And all the while, I kept an ear out for Sadie.

Tension was at an all-time high. The quick switch in her demeanor set everyone on edge. But once we got the security system installed, I knew things would clear up. Duke set Wren and me to the task of positioning the window sensors. Running lines along the floorboards. Setting up the Wi-Fi and Bluetooth connections in order to route calls through the main monitor at the doors. Sadie wanted a monitor at the front door as well as the back door. And I silently applauded her on her smart decisions.

Until I stuck my foot in my mouth.

"Thanks for your help, Duke. If you want to head out, I can walk Sadie through how to arm and disarm things in the morning," I said.

"Wait, wait, wait, wait. What?" Sadie asked.

I turned to look at her. "You know, in the morning. Once we leave for the airport? I can show you how to arm and disarm the house then."

"We won't have enough time to do that once you come get us. Duke can go over it with me now."

"I figured I'd be staying here, to make things easier."

She blinked. "I don't have anywhere to put you, Troy."

"I can sleep on the couch or something."

"And that didn't go over very well last time."

I furrowed my brow. "Are you saying you don't have space for me? Or that you don't want me staying here tonight with you? Because I figured with—"

"That's the issue. You figured. You didn't ask. You assumed."

"Well, given the situation we're in right now—"

"No, it's a situation *I'm* in. Not you."

I scoffed. "Seriously?"

"I'm being very serious. Look, you've been generous in what you're doing for me. But, I can handle this. I don't need you hovering over me all night while I'm trying to sleep and enjoy the last little bit of time my family's going to be here."

"Which you wouldn't have to enjoy if they simply stayed here to keep an eye on you."

"I don't need anyone keeping an eye on me. I'm a big girl with training underneath my belt. I can take care of myself."

I paused. "Where is this coming from right now?"

"It's coming from a place of truth. This isn't your issue to deal with, it's mine. You've trained me well. And if Luke does come looking for me, the last thing I want is yet another person in his path because of me."

"He's already been in my path, Sadie. And things turned out just fine."

"Exactly! But they might not turn out fine the next time."

"Which is why I want to be here. To protect you. To make sure he doesn't harm you."

She snarled. "He's already done that, Troy. And no one can change that."

"All right. All right. I think *every*one could benefit from taking some deep breaths. Yeah? Deep, slow, long breaths," Paris said.

Just as quickly as Sadie had switched into a personality I'd never seen before, it melted away. Shock took over her face as Paris guided her out of the room, followed swiftly by her parents. I looked over at Wren and all he could do was shrug. I looked over at Duke, and he did the same exact thing.

"What the absolute fuck was that?" I asked.

Yet, no one had an answer for me.

I did as she asked, though. I let her guide everything with Duke, then I left. As much as I hated it, I didn't stay with her that night. As much as I hated it, I got up earlier than the fucking sun and drove all the way back to her house to pick them all up. I hoped that, with some sleep, everyone might feel more refreshed. Less tense. Ready to take on the day and make it the best day possible, despite our current predicament.

But the tension was thicker than ever as I drove everyone to the airport.

We all rode in silence. No one looking at one another. Sadie, with her eyes staring out the window. She had her hands clasped between her thighs. Her leg, jiggling up and down maniacally. Something happened last night. I didn't know what, but I assumed by the scowl on her mother's face that a fight had ensued.

I pulled up to the airport's main doors and got out. With my car in park, I helped them haul their luggage out of my trunk. The hug between Sadie and her mother was terse. One-armed. Devoid of any emotion other than anger. Same with her father. One arm. No kiss. Just a basic hug to get through the civilities of the day.

"You guys have a safe flight. Let me know when you get home safely," Sadie said.

"How ironic," her mother murmured.

Sadie tossed her a curt smile. "Love you too."

I didn't know what to do. I didn't know how to fix things. And I'd never been in that kind of situation before. Where I couldn't fix shit. Where I didn't know what had to come next. This entire situation was one mind-blowing fuckery after the next, and it felt as if the snowball were getting bigger.

"Here, I can roll your luggage through the doors," I said.

I reached for Mrs. Powers' suitcases and she handed them to me.

"Thank you. That's very kind," she said.

I heard Sadie snicker as I ushered her parents into the airport.

"Troy?" her father asked.

I passed Mrs. Powers her luggage back. "Yes, sir?"

He held out a slip of paper. "I want you to call me and keep me up to date on Sadie. Okay?"

I took the piece of paper and unraveled it to find the man's phone number etched against it.

"Are you sure?" I asked.

"Our daughter is stubborn, Troy. For some reason, she always thinks that the world is out to suppress her. To take away her right to live her life as she sees fit. I don't know why she has that in her head, but she does," Mrs. Powers said.

I nodded. "I can call if you want me to, yes."

"Promise me, son," her father said.

His words hit me hard. No one had ever called me that. Other than my own mother, of course.

"I promise, sir. I'll call and keep you updated," I said.

"Preferably, as everything is happening and not weeks after the fact," she said.

I paused. "What?"

Her father chuckled. "We didn't even know her and Luke had broken things off until a week or so ago."

I looked out the window to see Sadie getting back into the car.

"You didn't?" I asked.

"No, we didn't," her mother said, "so, thank you for agreeing to do this."

"And please, keep our daughter safe. Even if she hates you in the moment for it," he said.

I slid the number into my pocket. "That, you can count on."

I gave them both hugs before I walked back out to the car. I slipped behind the steering wheel and felt the heat of Sadie's anger barreling toward me. I tried to shake it off, though. I knew she wasn't upset at us.

She was simply upset at how her life was being guided by some unseen punk-ass little rat bastard.

"What did they ask you to do?" she asked.

"I think you know," I said.

She snickered. "Figures."

"Well, had you told them sooner what was going on, they might not have felt the need to ask me to keep them updated."

"So, you're on their side now?"

"I'm on no one's side except the side that agrees to keep you alive, Sadie."

Silence filled the car as I pulled away from the curb.

"I know you hate what's going on right now—"

"How could you possibly understand what I'm going through right now?" she snipped.

"Because my ex stalked me after I broke up with her. That's why," I said.

I felt her looking at me. "Stalked you?"

I licked my lips. "It's a long story and I don't want to get into it. Just like you won't want to get into any of this Luke shit once it's past us. But, just know I understand. I get how old creeping around and looking over your shoulder gets. I understand how eerie nights can become. How weirded out even the brightest of corners can seem if you don't think you can fight your way out. And I get what you're doing. Pushing everyone away. I did the same thing when my ex was following me around everywhere."

"What do you mean?"

I sighed. "I pushed Wren away. Paris. I stopped going over to my mother's place. I did it because I thought I needed to do that in order to protect them. I felt my ex was a threat, and I didn't want them getting caught up in my bullshit. I see what you're doing. I know what it is you're doing. So, trust me when I tell you that isolating yourself is the exact thing he's wanting you to do right now. Because isolating yourself makes it easier for him to catch you alone. Giving him exactly what he wants."

I peeked over at Sadie and saw her eyes dancing along my face.

"Why didn't you ever tell me this before?" she asked.

I shrugged. "I guess for the same reason you only told your parents a week ago what all was happening?"

She snickered. "Because you didn't want to burden me with it?"

I nodded. "That, and I didn't want to worry you with everything else you've got on your plate."

"Why would that worry me?"

"Because you care about me. Because now—knowing that—I know you're thinking that you're reminding me of a terrible time in my life. Which is only going to fuel your want to push me further away. I won't let you do it, though. Because I care about you. And that's what people do when they care about each other. They worry about each other and borrow each other's toothpaste until one of them dies."

She giggled. "Seriously?"

I grinned. "Got a smile out of you, right?"

She settled back into her seat. "So, where are we headed?"

"Today, you're coming to the gym with me. And before you ask, yes. It is absolutely to keep you safe. I'd like to keep an eye on you today, for my sake. So, humor me, and you just might get a little surprise later."

"Oh, sounds like fun."

"It is. Especially if you like the saunas."

"Wait, what?"

I chuckled as I drove us to the gym. If I had *my* way? I'd make sure she was never alone again until Luke had been found. But, I knew that wasn't possible. Still, the promise of a fun time in the sauna had her walking into the gym at my side without a single amount of hesitation. And if I had to keep bartering sex just to keep her safe, I was more than willing to do that.

"Well, hello, hello. What do we have here? Did your parents get off to the airport okay?" Paris asked.

"Paris, meet our newest recruit for the day. Sadie will be helping us around the gym," I said.

"For a contracted fee of fourteen dollars an hour," Sadie said quickly.

I quirked an eyebrow. "And when were you going to mention this?"

She grinned. "Did you really think you'd get free labor out of me? I mean, really. Sex only goes so far, big boy."

"Oh, ho, ho! She's got jokes. I like jokes. You need to tell me more of these jokes while we go wash these nasty towels," Paris said.

"Please tell me there's at least decent coffee here," Sadie said.

Paris looped her arm around Sadie's. "It's not only good now, but it's never-ending."

"I'll take twelve an hour in exchange for all the coffee I can chug!" Sadie exclaimed.

I smiled. "Done!"

As I watched the two of them walk away, I thought back on the past few weeks. There was a time where it was only Mom and me. Before Paris came into the picture. Then, it was the three of us. Paris, myself, and Mom against the rest of the fucking world. Taking it on one swing at a time and defeating it with every blow of our fists. But Sadie? Uma? They had folded in nicely with our little family. Meshed well with us. In some ways, it felt like they had always been there. Which was why I had to keep them safe. Sadie, and Uma. All of us, really.

Because at this point, I didn't know what I'd do with my life if they weren't in it.

Sadie, especially.

"You done staring, Romeo?"

Mom's voice pulled me from my trance and I turned around.

"Good morning, Mom," I said.

"Good morning, Troy. If you're done, I could use an assist in my office. I've got Detroit Marketing on the phone. They want a conference call with us to iron out some things."

I looked down the hallway one last time. Just in time to see the girls disappear around the corner. And while I wanted to follow just to make sure no surprises cropped up, I knew Sadie was safe within these walls.

Especially with family surrounding her.

"Yeah, I'm done. Let's go," I said.

Though, I hoped I could convince her to let me stay the night tonight.

You know, just to keep an ear out for things while she slept.

Chapter 17

Sadie

"Do you want me to come stay with you tonight?"

"Did you arm your house before you left this morning?"

"You sure you don't want me to come by just until you go to sleep?"

"I really don't mind doing it. I miss you anyway."

"Sadie, quit being so stubborn. Just let me come over and stay. It'll help you feel better."

I wanted to punch Troy in his throat. His offer to "help" was becoming relentless. And with the incessant phone calls from my parents, I was ready to lock myself away until this entire nightmare was wrapped up. They were all getting on my nerves. Troy. Mom. Dad. Even Paris. The only person who seemed to not breathe down my throat about things was Uma.

But she was living with me.

So, maybe that was the reason why.

Even four days after they left, I was still frustrated with my parents. How they fought with me. How they insinuated that I couldn't take care of myself. The last thing I needed was a house full of people constantly fussing over me and giving me absolutely no space to live my life. The last thing I needed was for Luke to rip the last shred of dignity out of my life that I had to hold on to. It felt as if the world was against me right now. Every single part of it. Pushing against me and trying to knock me down and pin me into a place I didn't want to be.

I just had to keep reminding myself that no one really understood my position.

Not even Troy.

Though, he thinks he does.

I sighed as I sat at my desk. I stared at the email from my editor, taking in my next assignment. Some local seafood place on the outskirts of town. And the only person I really wanted to invite out with me was Uma. I reached for my cell phone and picked it up. I dialed her number, hoping and praying she was on a break from work.

And finally, the gods above smiled upon me.

"Well, hello lovely. What's shakin'?" Uma asked.

I smiled. "It's so good to hear your voice."

"Why? Bad day at work?"

"And thank you, for not automatically assuming it was related to Luke."

She snickered. "Troy and your parents still going at it?"

"Yeah. It seems unending. I've gotten used to ignoring the ringing of my phone."

"You know they only care about you and want to make sure you're okay."

"Yeah, well. I could do with about seven less phone calls a day."

"Why don't you try and find them something to do? Something that makes them feel as if they're contributing to keeping you safe?" she asked.

I shrugged. "Because there's nothing they can do."

"You could let Troy come stay over a night."

I groaned. "Not you. Please, not you, too, Uma."

"I guess I'm more curious as to why you don't want that big hunk of handsome man meat in your bed every night. That's the more concerning part to me."

I snickered. "It would be."

"So? What gives?"

I sighed. "I don't want anyone getting hurt because of me."

"Oh, come on, Sadie. You sound completely idiotic."

"Well, I don't! I mean, Luke's volatile. Unstable. And if something happens to someone, it's on me. It's my responsibility because I got them all wrapped up into this in the first damn place."

"This isn't your fault. You're smarter than that. This is all Luke's doing because he won't take no for an answer."

"Maybe so. But, that doesn't absolve me of the responsibility to protect those around me that I care about. Just like they want to make sure I'm safe, I want to make sure they're safe."

She giggled. "You just want to whip his ass by yourself."

"And make him bleed into the fucking sewers, girl."

She laughed. "All right, all right. I'm done pestering you about it. So, tell me. Did you call to ask me out on another one of these dates funded by your work?"

I grinned. "Oh, yes I did. You up for some seafood tonight?"

"Wait, tonight?"

"Oh no."

"Girl, why didn't you call me sooner than that?"

"I just got the email. What's up? Are you working another double or something?"

She whined. "I literally just got off the phone with someone saying I'd cover their shift tonight."

My head fell back in frustration. "Any way you can get out of it?"

"Nope. My word is my bond in this place. I'm sorry, girl. You got anyone else you can call?"

"I guess I could call Troy."

"You haven't called Troy yet?"

"We don't need to open that can of worms."

"Girl, get your head out of your ass and just talk to the man. Explain your side of things."

I pinched the bridge of my nose. "I have. And he's still up my ass about things."

"Well, then he cares. So, sue the guy."

I paused. "Will that really work?"

She snickered. "I have to go. Call him and try to be a reasonable person. Because I love you, but I'd like you to not go out to a restaurant at night with someone while Luke's still roaming about. Okay?"

I nodded. "Fair enough."

"Thanks. Love you lots."

"Love you too."

And after I hung up, I immediately called Troy.

"Sadie, are you okay? What's wrong? Where are you? I can come get you right—"

"Shit, will you take a breath for once?" I asked.

He sighed. "I'm sorry. It's the middle of the workday, so I figured—"

"I called to see if you wanted to come eat with me tonight. For work."

I closed my eyes as a pause fell over the line.

"What's for dinner?" he asked.

"This seafood place across town," I said.

"I can't do seafood."

"Wait, why not? You don't like it or something?"

"I have an allergy to shellfish. It's too risky, going into places like that to try and eat."

"How did I not know you had a shellfish allergy?" I asked.

He chuckled. "Well, you know now. But, you know who loves seafood?"

"Who?"

"Paris. You should give her a call. I'm sure she'd love to go with you."

I nodded. "All right. I'll give her a shot."

He sighed. "Do I dare ask if you want—?"

"No, Troy. I don't need you coming over to spend the night."

"Any way I can sway your mind on that?"

"No, Troy. There isn't any way you can sway my mind," I said flatly.

"You know I'm going to keep asking."

"And you know it's going to keep pissing me off."

"Yeah, well. At least I care."

"Yeah, well. Care from a distance. Because it's getting annoying."

Then, I hung up the phone.

"Ugh." I groaned.

I pressed the heels of my hands into my eyes. Did I really want to call Paris? Did I really want to deal with that all night? Because Troy wasn't actually the worst of it. She was. But, I knew I'd never hear the end of it if I didn't take someone to this restaurant. So, I picked up my phone and opened up a text to Paris.

Because I sure as hell didn't want to get back on the phone with anyone.

Me: Got a dinner job tonight. A seafood place on the other side of town. You wanna come with me tonight?

I sent it off to her and piddled around with work at my desk until my phone dinged.

Paris: Hell, yeah! I'm always down for seafood. Haven't met a fish I can't eat. Just name the time and place, and I'm there.

Me: Great :) the place is called Blalock's Seafood and Grill. They don't do reservations, so I was thinking six thirty for dinner? There's emphasis on trying their drink menu, so take a cab.

Paris: You don't have to tell me twice, lovely.

Oh, yes. Text messaging someone was a lot better.

Now that I had a dinner companion, I could focus on other things. Like editing articles, reshuffling information, and submitting possible places for me to write about to my editor. The day flew by with multiple phone calls from my parents gone unanswered. And as I stood up from my desk, my phone started ringing again. For the eighth time during my fucking workday.

"Hello, Dad," I said.

"Finally, you picked up. How are you doing?" he asked.

"I'm fine, Dad. I'm at work."

"How's it going? How are you feeling?"

I sighed. "I love you guys. I need you guys to know how much I love you. Because what I'm about to say next is going to sound harsh."

"I know, I know. You think we're calling—"

"I will get a new cell phone and a new number if you guys don't stop calling me at the top of every hour of every day."

"Sadie, I think you're being a little overdramat—"

"No, you're being overdramatic, Dad. You and Mom, both. I've been at work for six hours today and I have seven missed calls. Seven. This is the eighth call from you guys. I had to silence my phone just so other people around me could work."

"We're just worried about you. If you had let us stay up there with—"

"Had I let you stay up here, you would've been just as relentless, except it would've been face-to-face arguments rather than arguments over the phone."

I heard something rustling around on the other end of the line as I gathered my things.

"Sadie?"

I rolled my eyes. "Hey, Mom."

"First off, you will never address your father with that kind of disrespect ever again. Do you understand?"

I licked my lips. "Yep. I hear you."

"And secondly, we're worried about you. And you can't blame us for that. You have a man on the loose up there who has hurt you before and wants to do it again. If this was happening to Uma, or Paris, or anyone else? You'd be just as worried."

I made my way out the front doors. "I know, Mom. I know."

"So, instead of getting upset with us, answer our calls."

"I will, if it doesn't impede on the life I already lead. But, I can't answer one or two calls an hour because you guys are worrying about what may or may not be happening up here. This is happening to me. All of it is happening to me. And yet, I'm the only one who seems to be running my life as usual."

"And there's where you're wrong, sweetheart. When someone dies, does it affect *only* them?"

I snickered. "What?"

"When someone dies, Sadie, is the dead person the only one affected?"

"I, well, I mean, in a literal sense, sure."

"But, in a sense other than explicitly literal, does it affect only them?"

I sighed. "No."

"This situation doesn't just affect you. It affects every single person who cares about you. You've always been independent, and you've always felt as if you had to fight your own battles in order to prove something. But damn it, Sadie, we won't let you fight this one alone because this fight could get you killed. Do you hear me?"

I bit down onto my cheek. "Yes. I hear you."

"Good. Don't you dare let me hear you disrespecting your father like that again. And you better hope you're not speaking to Troy or anyone else up there like that. Because if you think you feel alone now? Wait until they walk away because of that attitude. Then, you'll really be alone. And you won't know what to do with yourself."

Tears brewed behind my eyes. "Read you loud and clear, Mom."

"Good. Now, how are you doing?"

I snickered. "I'm fine. I'm alive. No sign of Luke. But, I have a restaurant to attend tonight. I'm going with Paris. I need to catch a cab and go get dressed. I'll talk to you guys later."

And before my mother could get another word in edgewise, I hung up the phone.

Yeah, text messages were way fucking better than that.

I wiped away my tears as I got into my car. I had just enough time to get home, change, and get to the restaurant. Not the most convenient plan, but it would have to work for now. Until I could get a nice stash of clothes going at work to use for last-minute dinners like this one. I got home and changed into a nice pair of slacks and a long-sleeved blouse. I tucked it in, paired it with a slim yellow belt, and wore some matching yellow flats to pull it all together. Then, I threw my jacket back over my shoulders and headed straight for the other side of Detroit.

Where I found Paris waiting for me outside.

This was the first time the two of us would be alone for any long amount of time. And I wasn't sure what we had in common. Or, what we might talk about. But, I had to suck it up. I needed to get through this dinner in order to write and turn in my article tomorrow. Because I knew I'd go into work with another restaurant or spa or store or product I needed to try this week. The biweekly article formula seemed to work. Which meant doubling the amount of time I ran around doing stuff like this.

And while I loved it, even I had to admit that it made me vulnerable. Being out in public so much.

Which I didn't like.

"Hey, girl! Oh, love those shoes. Where'd you get them?"

I got out of my car and hugged Paris before we started into the restaurant.

"Uh, I've had them a while. Most of my shoes come from that discount outlet store, though," I said.

"The massive one that also sells the coats and mismatched socks?"

"I love those socks. I mean, they're so cute, even with their mismatched partners," I said.

"Right! I have, like, forty pairs of them. Wren teases me all the time about them, but I think they're great."

I smiled. "So, here's the plan for tonight. We have a different drink with every dish we order. No more than two entrees, one dessert each, and one appetizer each. Otherwise, we might raise some eyebrows. And the point is to keep a low profile."

"Got it. Anything specific you want me to get for us?"

"The only thing I've seen that I absolutely want to try are the—"

"Please say those steamed mussels for the appetizer. They look amazing."

I grinned. "That's exactly what I was going to say."

"Perfect, so, we get that and—"

"Can I help you two?"

The brash voice caught me off guard and I wondered who was speaking with us. I looked around the small entryway of the seafood place, but I didn't find anyone looking at us.

Except for the hostess.

"I'm sorry, what was that?" I asked.

"Do you two need help?" the woman asked curtly.

I looked over at Paris and she snickered.

"Uh, yes. We'd like a table for two," she said.

"Yeah, that's gonna take a bit. Name?" the hostess asked.

"Paris," she said.

I tossed her a silent thank you with my eyes as the woman scratched the name down at her podium.

"I'll call you when it's ready," she said.

"Do you know how long it might take?" I asked.

"I don't know. As long as it takes."

Paris scoffed and I sighed. Great. One of those places. And the hostess's attitude was only a foreshadowing of what was to come. While the food was outstanding, the service was horrible. No one had a good attitude about things. Everyone seemed to be in a rush, as if they were understaffed. And I saw multiple people flagging down the manager to complain about one thing or another.

To which the manager practically brushed them off.

"This place is a nightmare," Paris murmured.

"Which is a shame, because the food is great," I whispered.

"Right? I can't wait to take these leftovers home and feast on them later."

"Mine will be breakfast."

She wrinkled her nose. "Seafood for breakfast? Girl, you must have a stomach of iron."

"So I've been told."

"You guys want the check now?" our waiter asked.

I held out my hand. "Yes, please. Thank you so much."

"You guys need anything else? To-go drinks? Napkins? Anything like that?" he asked.

I shook my head. "Nope. Here's my card. Whatever the total is, is fine."

And when he saw the logo for Detroit Metro Times on the silver card, I thought the man was going to faint.

"Yes, of course. Right away," he said.

But, the sudden change in tone wouldn't save the restaurant in my review.

Because the public deserved to know how this restaurant treated their customers on a regular basis.

Chapter 18

Troy

The rumbling of the bike between my legs pulled me from my trance. I rode behind Wren, fighting the sting of the cold to enjoy my relaxing bike ride. Thursdays had become a new favorite day of mine. Not only because of seeing Sadie in class, but because of Wren's and my new riding day. Since the guys now got together every Monday after work down by the lake, we shifted our personal riding day to Thursdays. After self-defense. As a way to wind down before going to get us some much-needed food.

But my mind was preoccupied.

Other than a soft kiss from Sadie after self-defense class tonight, I hadn't seen her all week. I hated letting her be alone like that. Always looking out for herself. Going anywhere and everywhere alone. It killed me that I couldn't suck it up enough to go to that restaurant with her a couple of nights back. Mom would've killed me, though. Knowing I had gone to a seafood place like that. I almost agreed, though, because Sadie and I hadn't gotten much time to spend together lately.

And that, alone, was killing me softly.

"Hey, dude, you good?"

My microphone came alive in my ear and I heard Wren's voice filling it.

"Yeah, I'm good."

"You getting hungry? I can turn around and get us back to Joe's."

I snickered. "You know I'm always ready for wings and beer. But, you really want to do Joe's with how busy it's been lately?"

Wren chuckled. "You know Thursdays are his slow-ass day."

"Well, let's go see just how slow-ass it is, then. Because I've been craving those wings now for days."

I wanted, more than anything, for these bike rides to calm me down. To relax me. To breathe new life into my haggard body. But, I knew I wouldn't rest easy until Luke was caught again. I kept myself from asking Wren about it. I had beat the damn topic to death. And every time I brought it up, he got frustrated talking about it.

Especially since they didn't have any leads on where the asshole went.

Wren held out his arm to the left before whipping a sharp turn. I held my leg out and followed him around the tight corner, then the two of us sped off into the back alleys. Dodging around tipped-over trash cans and rushing through piles of garbage, we soared behind buildings. Evading traffic in order to get to our food a little quicker. I drew in the harsh, cold air. I sank into the rhythmic thrumming of the bike between my legs. I tried to let myself go. Let my mind wander. Let my spirits soar.

But I was forever chained to my worry.

Forever chained to the constant question of whether or not Sadie was all right.

Wren pulled into the parking lot of Joe's and I saw it had been repaved. It wasn't full, though. Which was a good sign. We parked our bikes in their usual spots. Then, with our helmets tucked underneath our arms, we headed inside.

And the smell of disinfectant caught me off guard.

"What the fuck?" I asked.

Wren snickered. "Damn. Guess they're actually cleaning the place now."

Joe's looked almost spotless. A few of the booth seats had been fixed. And the rest of them had been completely replaced. The bar glistened with a hue I'd never seen before. The black walls and black floor had a shimmer to them that was new to me. I slowly looked over at

Wren and he shrugged. But, before we could make our way to our regular seats, a very cheery girl came up to us.

One I didn't recognize.

"Hi there! Welcome to Joe's. You guys can sit anywhere you want and I'll be right with you. Okay?"

I nodded slowly. "Yeah. Okay."

"Well, you heard the girl. Let's go take a seat."

I searched the bar for our old pal, but he was nowhere to be found. We made our way to our regular seats in the corner, and the cushions felt, well, softer than the last time we had sat on them. Apparently, this place was really doing something with the money they were raking in. And while change was sometimes a good thing, I wondered if Joe's would end up becoming another one of those uppity places where the portions eventually grew too small and the lines for dinner constantly wrapped around the corner of the building.

"So, how are you and Sadie doing?"

Wren's question snapped me from my trance. "Why don't we start with how you and Paris are doing."

"That good, huh?"

"Humor me. No one's really doing that lately."

He snickered. "Well, I mean, we're doing great actually. Got a nice routine going. Certain nights at her place, certain nights at mine. Hell, we've even got our own pizza-and-movie night."

"That's some pretty serious shit."

"Yeah, man. Especially for me. I've never made it this far with a woman."

I blinked. "You were hooking up with a girl for almost nine months one time."

"Yeah, hooking up. Nothing like this, though, dude. Paris is different. She's special. I just hope I make her feel that way."

I grinned. "I see the way she smiles at you. You're doing something right."

"Don't know what the fuck it is. But, I'm lucky it's working."

"I think Paris fits you well, too, because she doesn't need fancy things in order to feel good about herself. That helps you out a lot."

"And thank fuck for it. Because I never figured out that fancy romantic shit like you did."

I shrugged. "Eh, the fancy romantic shit gets old after a while. Especially when it's not appreciated or reciprocated."

"Does Sadie like it?"

"Like what?"

"The fancy romantic shit?"

I thought she did. "I haven't stepped into that territory with her yet."

"Why not?"

Because she doesn't even want me around. "You of all people know she's got a lot on her plate right now."

He shrugged. "Maybe some fancy romantic shit would help get her mind off things."

Or, it'll push her further away. "I'll think about it."

"You know, Paris and I were talking the other day about taking a weekend away together soon."

"Oh? Where to?"

He shrugged. "I don't know. We didn't get that far. But we figured if we can spend a weekend here together with each other, maybe it's time to try taking a weekend away from here. Like, a cabin somewhere. Or going to see Niagara Falls."

I grinned. "She's always wanted to see that place."

"I know! I've heard her mention it a few times. I kind of wanna surprise her with it. But, I kind of want her to be in the planning process too. You know, so I don't screw it up."

"You know you can buy open-ended tickets to the Falls, right?"

He blinked. "What?"

"Yeah. You can buy a ticket and use it whenever you want. So, maybe surprise her with the tickets, and then the two of you plan the weekend to go."

He leaned forward. "You're a fucking genius, dude."

"Hi there! Sorry, guys. Had to deal with a little mess. What can I get you guys started on? The bacon cheese fries here are to die for!"

The cheery girl reappeared at our side and I wrinkled my nose.

"Bacon cheese fries?" I asked.

"Oh, yes. They're new, and ah-mazing. Waffle fries, fried twice, then run through a stone oven with three types of cheeses and crispy bacon on top. Served with our in-house ranch dressing. It's so good. You really need to try them," she said.

"In-house ranch?" Wren asked.

"I helped tweak the recipe," the girl said proudly.

Wren and I slowly looked at each other before we shrugged.

"Uh, sure. Let's do an order of that for us to split, then I'm gonna do twenty original hot wings and a beer."

"Same order here," he said.

"Wonderful. What kind of beer?" the girl asked.

I blinked. "Just whatever beer you got."

"Well, we have twelve on tap, four in bottles, and six in cans. Our menu's right there on the table, if you'd like to take a look at it."

I slowly looked over at Wren and he shrugged.

"Uh, yeah. Give us a second," I said.

"Sure thing. I'll put this order in and be right back," the girl said.

"There's a beer menu now?" Wren whispered.

I shrugged. "I mean, if it's working for them, I guess."

"Looks like Joe's is moving up in the world."

"Good for them," I said.

He plucked the beer menu from behind the salt and pepper and held it up. He scanned the front while I scanned the back. Then, he flipped it around for me to take in the front. I didn't really care about the beer, so long as it didn't taste like piss. They had a couple of nice stouts I wanted to try, though. So, when the girl came back over to our table, we placed our drink orders.

Before Wren hit me with a stark question.

"Does it strike you as odd, how close we all got to each other so quickly?"

I thought on his question hard. "I've been curious about that lately."

"You think it's weird?"

I shrugged. "I mean, sometimes you just know, right? It just clicks."

"Like we've always been a group."

I nodded. "Yeah. At least, it feels that way."

"Well, I'm glad I'm not the only person who feels that way about things."

"You're not."

"You think Paris would wait to go to Niagara Falls after this shit with Sadie is wrapped up?"

I grinned. "I don't think Paris would want to leave for a weekend without it being wrapped up either."

"So, we all stick around until Luke's caught. Then, weekend trip."

I nodded. "Sounds like a plan."

"Good. Good. All right. That makes me feel better."

And as the cheery waitress-slash-hostess-slash-ranch-enthusiast brought our drinks to us, I settled back into the booth. Finally relaxing as I filled my stomach with the incredible dark stout. It made me feel good, knowing our group was hesitant about leaving town with Sadie being so vulnerable. And while I knew she wouldn't like the idea of us putting things like this on hold for her, what she didn't know wouldn't hurt her.

Except for wherever the hell Luke is right now.

Chapter 19

Sadie

I heard my cell phone ringing and rolled over in bed. I groaned as I reached for it, ready to chew out whoever the hell was calling me so early on a damn Saturday morning. I pressed the flashing green button and held the damn phone to my face. Another call, another fight, another person to talk down from some frivolous high of always needing to check up on me because I was apparently incapable of operating on my own. Ever.

"Hello?" I asked groggily.

"Good morning, sleepyhead."

I furrowed my brow. "Miss Katie?"

She snickered. "Pretty sure we're at a point where you can just call me Katie. Or Ma."

I sat up in bed. "What are you doing calling me so early? Is everything okay?"

"Early? Sadie, it's half past eleven."

"It's what?"

I pulled the phone away from my face and looked at the time. Holy shit. It was 11:34 in the morning.

"You okay?" Troy's mother asked.

"Yeah, yeah. Just, apparently very tired," I said.

I flopped back down into bed and cleared my throat.

"Well, I was just calling to let you know that you're still more than welcome in the beginning kickboxing class, even though you came to the intermediate class this week. And to tell you that the self-defense class is still on for tonight, despite the ice warning we're supposedly under."

"Ice warning?"

"It rolled through about an hour ago."

I sighed. "Gotcha. Okay. Good to know."

"But, if you just want to stop by the gym and hang out, you can do that too. You're welcome anytime."

I grinned. "So you can keep an eye on me?"

"Nope. So you can have a place where you feel safe. That's all."

"Uh-huh."

"Take it for what it's worth, Sadie. Nothing more, nothing less."

I sighed. "Well, I do appreciate it. Thank you."

"And if you do decide to come in, can you snatch me up some doughnuts? I didn't have time to get any when I first came in this morning, and I've got a serious craving."

I giggled. "Doughnuts. Got it. Any particular ones?"

"Oh, Dunkin' Donuts always has the best. Troy always insists on going to little specialty shops, but nothing beats their sour cream doughnuts. Or their blueberry ones."

"Sour cream doughnut?"

She paused. "Are you kidding me right now?"

"What's a sour cream doughnut?"

"Okay. Yep. When you get the doughnuts—*if* you get them—get yourself one too. Trust me on this, and you can thank me later."

I giggled. "Noted."

"All right. Hopefully, I'll see you later on today."

"And the doughnuts."

"Those too. But, mostly you. Like, sixty percent you."

I barked with laughter. "Sixty percent. Got it."

I hung up the phone with Miss Katie and lay there, staring up at the ceiling. On the one hand, I knew Troy would be at the gym most of the day. Which meant the possibility that he'd be shoved up my ass.

On the other hand, though, we hadn't seen a lot of each other. And any chance to ogle my boyfriend was a good idea. Especially with those tattoos. And those muscles.

And the way his skin glistens in the sauna.

"Yep. All right. To the gym, we go." I grunted.

I rolled myself out of bed and slowly got ready for the day. If I was going to head to the gym, I'd make an entire day out of it. I reached for my purse and started folding up some clothes to jam straight to the bottom. My workout clothes for the night, a set of pajamas just in case the ice caught me at a bad time, and my laptop. Because I never went anywhere without that thing. I packed a miniature overnight bag for the worst-case scenario, then headed into the bathroom.

And after quickly cleaning myself up, I made my way downstairs.

"Uma, you up?" I asked.

"Finally. I was about to come up there and take your damn pulse," she said.

I giggled. "I'm headed to the gym for the day. So, I'll see you for classes tonight."

"You know there's an ice warning, right?"

"Well, then I might not see you for classes tonight."

"You got yourself packed up in case you can't get back?" she asked.

I held up my bag. "Got everything I need for an overnight, if it's necessary."

I walked over and gave Uma a hug. Then, I walked into the kitchen. I made myself a tumbler of coffee to take with me, knowing damn good and well I'd have to take it slow anyway. For some reason, I still felt tired. Even though I'd been asleep for well over twelve hours, my body still felt as if it were dragging.

Honestly, I'd felt like that ever since my seafood outing with Paris.

Damn, that food really did a number on me.

"Okay, Uma, I'm heading out!" I exclaimed.

"Love you, mean it, call me when you get to the gym!"

"And hopefully I'll see you tonight!"

I headed straight for my car, and the cold perked me up quickly. I shivered and shook as I rushed to my car, desperate to get inside. Fucking hell, I should've worn something a bit thicker than yoga pants and a cardigan. Still, though, I had an emergency scarf and hat in my car I tossed on. Which helped keep me somewhat sane as I sipped my hot coffee.

Waiting for my freezing cold car to warm up.

When I was convinced my car wouldn't fall apart if I moved it, I made my way into town. And the first Dunkin' Donuts I came upon, I pulled into the drive-through. I did as Katie asked. I got myself a sour cream doughnut. And while I wasn't sure what to expect, the damn thing still caught me off guard.

"Holy shit, this is good," I murmured.

I devoured my doughnut on the way to the gym. Chasing it down with coffee somehow made it taste better. And suddenly, I was glad I had gotten four of those damn things in the dozen I bought. I pulled into a parking space and gathered up all my things. With my coffee in one hand and the doughnuts balanced in the other, I walked as gingerly as I could. Because every time my heavy purse swung, it threatened to knock me off-balance.

"Oh my gosh. Let me help you," Katie said.

She rushed out from behind the welcome desk and swept in to take the doughnuts. I shifted my purse back onto my shoulder and shot her a grateful look. She opened the box and stuck one of those dreamy doughnuts between her teeth. Then, she closed the box and smiled.

"You're awesome," she said with her mouth full.

I giggled. "Come on. Let's go hide those in your office before someone finds them."

"I like how you think."

I followed her to her office, where I beckoned for another sour cream doughnut. She shot me an I-told-you-so look. But, I didn't mind it. Because she really did. The thing was outstanding, and I wanted as many of them as I could get.

Good thing I came to the gym today.

"If you're looking for him, Troy's in the free-weight room. Otherwise, the classroom studio is empty. If you want to get a little sweat on yourself," Katie said.

I smiled. "Thanks. My first stop is to shove this stuff in my locker. Then, I'm thinking of kicking up a sweat myself."

"Perfect. I'll make sure the door's unlocked."

I made my way to the locker room and the saunas were already calling me. I hadn't even done anything, and already I wanted to relax in them. What was wrong with me today? It was like I couldn't jump-start my body. I shoved my things into my locker and closed the door, spinning the dial of the lock a few times. Just to make sure no one could get into it.

And as I made my exit, I didn't turn to go toward the classroom.

I turned to go toward the free-weight room.

Before I knew it, I stood there. In the doorway. Ogling Troy as he lifted himself up on the pull-up machine. His arms dripped with sweat. He had his legs locked, which made his muscles bulge. His veins twitched. He grunted softly, sending shivers of electricity down my spine. And as I licked my lips, I drank in the artwork that was Troy's body.

Every inch of him was etched in strength. Streaked with sweat. The outlines of his muscles were seen through the clothes that stuck to him like glue. Preening him for my viewing pleasure. I crossed my arms over my chest because I felt my nipples hardening. I leaned against the doorway of the room because I felt my knees weakening. With every grunt of his that got louder, my stomach clenched. Every soft curse that fell from his lips made me quiver with need for him.

And when he dropped down to his feet, his eyes quickly found mine.

I watched him as he crossed the room. Walking with determination, and purpose, and pride. He grinned at me as he grew closer, his musky scent filling my nostrils. I pressed my back against the wall. My neck craned back to keep his face in view. His arm reached out for me and I thought he was going to pull me into the sweatiest hug imaginable.

Until his lips fell to mine in a searing kiss.

"Mmm, Troy."

My hands pressed softly against his chest. I slid them over his shoulders, feeling how he twitched for me. I stood on my tiptoes, crashing myself against him. Wanting nothing more than to taste all of him. His body pressed me back against the wall. His hands roamed my body. I fisted his damp shirt, pulling him even closer as my tongue fell down the back of his throat.

Causing him to growl.

Which made my toes curl in my tennis shoes.

"Wasn't sure you were coming in today, beautiful," he murmured.

I smiled as my forehead fell against his. "Well, here I am."

"I'm glad you're here. How long are you staying?"

I shrugged. "Maybe for an hour. Maybe through class. Who knows, really."

He chuckled. "And what made you decide to come in today?"

"I mean, any chance to see you looking like a men's health magazine sounds like a good time to me."

I giggled at my own joke before he tackled me quickly to the mats. And our only saving grace was the fact that no one was in the free-weights room other than us. His body pressed itself between my legs, shrouding me in his sweaty nature. Our teeth clattered together with the force of our kiss, and I felt more alive than ever before. I rolled my hips against him. I wrapped my arms tightly around his neck. I bucked my hips and felt him groan before I quickly rolled him over onto his back.

"Wow. Seems you're really retaining stuff from class," he said breathlessly.

"I guess I just have a really good teacher," I whispered.

"Oh, yeah? Well, can you remember how to get out of this?"

He slipped from underneath me and pinned me onto my stomach. With my wrists wrapped around behind my back, his lips fell to my ear. Breathing softly. Taunting me with kisses. Egging me on like the beautiful bastard he was.

"What do you do now?" He breathed.

But, before I could try the new maneuver from our last class, a whistle caught my ear.

"Let me know when the next fight happens. I wanna sell tickets to the show," Miss Katie said.

My cheeks turned four versions of cherry red as Troy scrambled off my body. He helped me to my feet as his mother walked by, munching on a doughnut and winking at us both. I buried my face in my hands. Troy let out a small groan. And as she walked down the hallway, I sighed.

"Your mother's a straight-up menace," I said.

"Trust me, I know," he said.

"I heard that!" Miss Katie exclaimed.

"Good!" Troy yelled.

But, it didn't stop him from taking me in his arms again and kissing me with a fury that left me breathless.

Nor did it stop me from feeling every inch of his pulsing muscles with my fingertips while I had the chance.

Chapter 20

Troy

"So, as you can see, the first stage of this new rollout for our advertising consists of the billboards. We want to get a feel for how you'd like your gym represented on the three going up around Detroit," Kurt said.

"Three billboards?" Mom asked.

He nodded. "Yep. Three in Detroit, one just outside of Washington, and one on the highway just as people come into Michigan from the south. That one won't be up until the end of the year, but these other four will be up by the end of the month. We've got three main ideas we're bouncing between. Let us know what you think."

Mom looked at me and I saw the excitement in her face. Kurt—Wren's brother—had done a fantastic job talking us through how this new advertisement rollout was going to look. The money we were saving with this kind of thing was mind-blowing too. Being guinea pigs was paying off, for sure.

"All right, so this is the first one. It's an advertisement within an advertisement. So, remember that. It's just a matter of getting the right feel," Kurt said.

"I'm ready when you are," Mom said.

The first billboard that flashed up on the screen made me wrinkle my nose. It was terrible. The people were much too big, the logo for the gym was much too small, and for some reason it had our old color scheme on it.

"You know those aren't the colors for our gym, right?" Mom asked.

Kurt paused. "They're not?"

I shook my head. "Nope. We're not purple and orange any longer. We're orange, pale yellow, and black."

Kurt nodded slowly. "Huh. Well, that's going to make this meeting more interesting."

"Troy, didn't you email the man?" Mom asked.

"Not Kurt specifically. I emailed his—"

My phone started ringing on my hip and I wanted to melt into the damn floor. I felt my face pale as I reached for it deep within the wells of my suit pocket. I silenced it immediately, trying to focus on a meeting that was already spiraling down the drain. Plus, with Mom shooting daggers at me from her eyes, I knew she was about to lose her footing with this thing anyway.

Which meant I had to step up to the plate.

"Can you tell me exactly who you sent the email to?" Kurt asked.

"Mrs. Brinkley? In Design. I sent her our updated website, the template for the updated color scheme, and our updated logo," I said.

"So, this isn't even what your logo looks like anymore," he said.

I shook my head. "No. It's not."

He sighed. "Well, it seems as if we have a great deal of tweaking to do. I'm sorry to have wasted your time."

"Um, excuse me. I'm sorry to interrupt. But, Troy?"

I slowly turned around at the sound of Paris's voice.

"Can it wait?" I asked.

"It can't. It's Sadie," she said.

"Sadie?" Mom asked.

"Who's Sadie?" Kurt asked.

I shot up from my chair. "Paris, what's wrong?"

"She's in the hospital, Troy. Uma tried calling you before she called me. She just rolled into the ER about—"

I whipped around. "I'm sorry. You'll have to excuse me. My girlfriend's been hurt."

Kurt stood. "Of course. Go, go. Miss Katie, if you don't mind staying with me, we can at least get input on what style billboard you guys want. Then, I can get you mock-ups at the end of the week for—"

Mom waved me on. "Go. I've got this."

I strode to Paris. "Stay with Mom. Help her with this meeting. You know as much as I do on this. I have to go."

"Text me, okay?"

I nodded. "Of course."

I raced out of the building and headed straight for my car. I sped like a bat out of hell, trying to get to the hospital as quickly as I could. My heart pounded in my chest. It felt like my world had just come crashing down over my head. I didn't like this. I didn't like the way this felt, or smelled, or sounded. I white-knuckled the steering wheel as I careened into the parking lot. And as I ran for the emergency room doors, only one thought crossed my mind.

Did Luke get to her again?

"Sir? Sir, can I help—sir!"

I felt a nurse grab me by the arm and I whipped around.

"Sadie Powers. She just came in a little while ago. I know the nurse who brought her in. Or is here with her. Uma...?"

"It's okay, Chora. I know him. I've got him," Uma said.

Relief poured through my veins. "Tell me you know something."

She took my hand. "Follow me. Come on. We need to get you calmed down."

"Uma, I'm not going to be calm until you give me—"

She glared at me. "Shut up and come on."

I did as she asked as she tugged me into a corner. We sat down in a couple of chairs tucked away by a water fountain that was out of order. I looked around at the people walking by us. Seemingly unaware of how much I was shaking. There were women crying. Men looking scared. Children coughing up a storm and others sneezing in the distance. The place was a damn madhouse. And Sadie was somewhere inside.

"Tell me what you know. Please," I said.

Uma took my hands. "We had to triage her. Sadie's pretty hurt."

"What happened to her?"

"We're still not sure. She came in unconscious. One minute, I'm stitching up a boy who wanted to run with a colored pencil in his hand, and the next minute I've got someone replacing me because they want me in another room. I get there, it's Sadie, and my first instinct was to call you."

"How bad is it?"

She swallowed hard. "Bad enough that I had to tag someone in to work on her because I couldn't do it myself."

I clenched my jaw. "It was him, wasn't it?"

She shook her head. "I don't know. We've got no way of knowing what happened until Sadie wakes up."

"He beat her, didn't he?"

"See, that's the thing. She doesn't look beaten."

"Then, what does she look like, Uma? Give me something."

"She looks ... buried."

I blinked. "Buried?"

She nodded. "Yeah. Like ... like scrapes on her face. No real impact points. Just a lot of bystanding damage. I don't know how else to explain it."

"So, it wasn't Luke."

"I don't know. I really don't. I took a few seconds' worth of a look at her before I determined I couldn't work on my best friend, Troy."

I stood and pulled her upright with me.

"Thank you for calling me," I said.

"Of course. Yeah. Of course, I'd call you," she said.

I pulled her in for a hug and sighed heavily. Uma held me tightly in that corner while the two of us waited. My Sadie. Unconscious. In a room, all by herself. It made me sick to think about. But, if an ambulance brought her here, to this hospital, then it meant that whatever happened most likely happened at work.

Maybe I should call up there.

"Sadie Powers?"

Uma ripped out of my grasp. "Yes. We're with her. Is she awake?"

The nurse nodded. "You two can come on back. I take it that's the boyfriend."

She nodded. "Yep. This is him. Lead the way, Shelley."

Uma tugged me through a massive set of steel doors. We walked down the long corridors, filled with crying children, worried parents, and vomiting patients. It felt as if the emergency room was never-ending. I held Uma's hand tightly, refusing to lose her as her walking sped up. Until we were practically jogging to the very far end room on the left.

"She's in here. Though, you need to be quiet. She was complaining of her head hurting when she first came to," the nurse said.

"Thanks," Uma whispered.

"Concussion?" I asked.

The nurse shrugged. "We won't know until she can talk more to us. But, we are on a concussion watch, yes."

I sighed. "Thank you. For all you did."

I walked behind Uma into the room and Sadie's appearance stunned me. She had a wrap around her wrist and a bandage circling all the way around her head. Covering one of her eyes. Uma sat on the edge of her bed, holding her good hand. And as I crept around to the other side, I pulled up a chair.

While taking in the scrapes and bruises that cascaded in long, sharp lines down her body.

"Sadie," I murmured.

She tried turning her head toward me, but she winced.

"Troy?" she asked.

I laid my hand against her bandaged forearm. "Yeah, it's me. I'm here."

"Troy," she whispered.

"Sadie, can you tell us what happened?" Uma asked.

She swallowed hard. "It's still kind of hard to remember. But, uh..."

I drew in a ragged breath. "Just tell us what you can. That's good enough."

"I um, my car wouldn't start when I got out to it. I mean, for lunch. I don't know why. The tank had gas. It worked fine this morning," Sadie said.

"What did you do after that?" Uma asked.

"It was too cold to walk to get anything for lunch. So, I figured I'd take a bus ride. You know, down to that deli?"

"Makes sense," I said.

"The next thing I know, I hear tires skidding. People at the bus stop moving out of the way. Then, the thing comes down on top of me."

"What thing?" Uma asked.

"The bus stop," she said.

"You mean, the awning that you sit under to wait for the bus?" I asked.

Sadie nodded slowly. "Yeah. Some car hit it and it came down on me. Just like that."

I looked over at Uma. "Is there any possible way this could've been Luke?"

Uma shot me a worried glance before we both turned our eyes back to Sadie. And when my beautiful, sweet woman didn't answer immediately, I knew she was thinking the same thing.

"I mean, I didn't see him. But, I do feel like the cops should know what's happened. So they know to keep an eye out for him, just in case," she said softly.

"Someone need an officer?"

We all turned and looked at the paunch security guard standing in the doorway. Nurse Shelley was behind him, and all she did was nod. I turned my attention back to Sadie and I saw her shivering. Which caused Uma to tuck her in tighter with another blanket.

I knew it wouldn't help, though. Because Sadie wasn't shivering from the cold.

"Yes, Officer. I believe we do need one," I said.

If I didn't hate the man before, I did now. If I really didn't want to kill the man before, I knew I'd smile all the way to prison if I got the chance to do it now. The officer nodded for me to get up before he spoke into the radio on his shoulder. I wasn't sure what he could do in this situation. But, it couldn't hurt to shoot a text off to Wren and let him know what was going on.

So, as I got up from my chair, I did just that.

Me: Wren, Sadie's in the hospital. She was sitting at a bus stop near her work. Said a car came charging for the bus stop and it collapsed on top of her. I want your hands in that scene. Also, check her car at work. I think it might've been tampered with. Don't ask why. Please.

Chapter 21

Sadie

"No, sir, I didn't actually see him at the bus stop."

"Yes, sir, I just want to make the police aware of what's happened, in case it was him."

"All I know is he hasn't been caught yet. So, he's out there."

"No, I didn't see who was driving the car."

I gave my account to the security guard standing at the side of my bed. But, I could tell he wasn't very amused with the situation. I didn't care, though. I hurt everywhere and my wrist had been dislocated. Which meant no using it for a few weeks. Couple that with the pain in my skull—and the fact that my eye had been swollen shut—and I was a recipe for exactly what *shouldn't* happen to a journalist.

I'd have to rely on my dictation software to get me by for a while.

The hospital went by in a blur. The pain muted most everything until the pain medication kicked in. Then, it made me so tired I couldn't pay attention anyway. I heard Uma say something about "getting her car" and Troy quipped back with something about "checking it out."

Coincidences, maybe?

I didn't know. I just wanted to go home and sleep.

"All right, let's get you into this wheelchair. Troy, you come around with your car and I'll get her into the seat," Uma said.

"Home," I murmured.

She kissed the top of my head. "Yes, pretty girl. That's where we're headed. Home. And I've got some time off to help you get back on your feet."

"That's ... okay..."

The next thing I remembered was Uma helping me out of Troy's car. Helping me inside the house. Helping me sit down at the kitchen table. The smell of grits lingered in the air, making my stomach growl. But, my head kept falling forward. My body felt heavy.

"Sleep?" I asked.

"Let's get some food in you first," Troy said.

I jumped at his voice. "Where did you come from?"

He chuckled. "I drove the car to get you home. Now, are you okay to eat? Or, do I need to feed you?"

I raised my good hand. "I'm not completely helpless."

My vision started doubling because of how tired the pain medication made me and I had to close my eyes to find the spoon. I scooped up some of the hot grits and brought it slowly to my mouth. Before I felt something hot plop into my lap. I jumped and the chair scooted backward. I felt someone's hands come down against my shoulders. Panic rose up the back of my throat and tears rushed my eyes before I felt a hand cup my cheek.

"It's okay. It's just me and Uma. You dropped the grits in your lap. Hold still. I'm trying to clean you up."

Troy's voice soothed me as a tear slipped from the corner of my unwrapped eye.

"Sorry," I whispered.

"No need to be sorry. Just hold still, okay?" he asked.

After giving over control of my food to him, he fed me. Bite, after bite, after bite. Until the bowl of cheesy grits was gone and my water had been downed. On the one hand, I didn't like feeling that helpless. That out of control. That insecure with everything. But, on the other hand, having Troy dote on me felt good. Especially when he wasn't judging me for it.

"I'm sorry," I whispered.

"You have no reason to apologize," he said.

"I'm sorry for pushing you away."

"Sadie, it's okay."

"I'm sorry for always—"

He scooped me up from the chair. "Trust me, you don't want to apologize yet."

I paused. "Why's that?"

"Because I promised your parent's I'd keep them updated."

I felt myself grow cold inside. He set me on the couch and got me wrapped up in a blanket before walking away. Before backtracking somewhere in the house. To call my fucking parents. I shook my head as I lay down. As I tried to get comfortable. I let the tears freely fall as I shivered against the couch.

"You running a fever?" Uma asked.

Her hand fell against my forehead before she sighed.

"He made a promise to your parents. And you know he's not the kind of man to break a promise," she said.

"Yeah. I know," I said flatly.

I wanted to be mad at him. I really did. But, with the pain medication came a drop in my defenses. And I felt reason taking over. My parents were worried. I'd just been in the hospital. Of course, someone had to call them. I mean, if I had a kid and this was happening to them, I'd want to know all about it. Hell, I'd probably stay in town, even if my kid didn't want me to! Get a hotel room somewhere to be close, just in case.

"I've been such a bitch," I whispered.

"All right. How's she doing?" Troy asked.

Uma giggled. "I think she's finally coming around."

I sniffled. "Troy?"

I felt him sit down and pull my legs into his lap.

"What's up, beautiful?" he asked.

"Thank you for keeping your promise to my parents," I said.

He paused. "Uh, well, you're ... you're welcome, Sadie."

Uma sputtered with laughter. "I'm going to go make us some hot chocolate. You guys want anything else?"

"Sleep," I murmured.

"Hot chocolate sounds great. Thanks, Uma," he said.

"I'm so sorry I've been a nightmare," I whispered.

Troy smoothed his hand up and down my leg. "Don't be sorry. Just let us help. That's all we want."

"Troy! Sadie!"

I heard the front door burst open, causing Uma to cry out. I jerked against Troy as he quickly stood up, as if adrenaline rushed through his veins. It took me a second to register Wren's voice. Register it as him booming through the house.

"I've got news! It wasn't Luke! The bus stop wasn't Luke!"

I sat up. "Wren, bring it down a couple notches."

Troy cleared his throat. "And you're sure about that?"

I finally got my good eye to open long enough to see Wren storm into the living room. His movements frantic and his smile lopsided.

"We're very sure. We've got footage of it and everything. The woman who hit the bus shelter had a heart attack while she was driving. She lost consciousness behind the wheel of her car. It wasn't Luke," he said.

"Holy shit, is she all right?" I asked.

"I never thought I'd be so relieved to hear about a heart attack," Uma said.

"She's going to be just fine. At least, the hospital says she will be," Wren said.

"So, no sign of Luke at all?" Troy asked.

Wren shook his head slowly. "Fortunately, and unfortunately, no."

I nodded slowly. "Thank you for coming out all this way to tell me."

"Well, in my defense, I tried calling everyone's cell phones. Apparently, no one wants to pick them up today."

I snickered. "I'm getting a bit sick of cell phones, myself."

Troy chuckled. "That a jab at me?"

"It's a jab at everyone, as far as I'm concerned."

And as I lay back down, I allowed myself to drift off to sleep. With Troy, Wren, and Uma talking around me. I mean, I trusted them. I trusted them to be in my home, even though I wasn't awake. I didn't have to worry while they were around. Plus, I needed the rest before I tackled the phone call with my editor.

Because I knew he wouldn't be happy to hear about this.

Chapter 22

Troy

I sighed as I leaned back into my office chair with my cell phone propped against my shoulder. I should've called him sooner than this. Especially with this gym that meant so much to me. I had worked much too hard with my mother on this place to let an opportunity like this marketing deal slip through my fingers. But, Sadie was more important at that moment.

However, I still felt as if I owned Kurt an apology.

"DTM, this is Kurt."

"Kurt, it's Troy."

"Hey! I'm glad I've got you on the phone. My design team has already finished the billboard in the two styles your mother chose at our last meeting. I'm about to send them your way. Care to give me some on-the-spot feedback?"

I blinked. "I mean, that's fine. But I really wanted to call and—"

"Perfect. I'll copy your mother's email on them and get them right to you."

"Kurt, what happened at the meeting—"

"Our logo is still a bit larger, well, because it needs to be. With the project and all. But, I think you're going to be very happy."

I snickered. "Are you going to let me apologize?"

"No, I'm not."

I paused. "Why not?"

"At the expense of possibly getting my little brother in trouble, you don't have to."

I sighed. "Ah."

"Yeah."

"You know."

"Troy, don't get upset with him. Wren was concerned about things when he found out—"

"How much do you know?"

A pause fell over the phone, kneading my stomach into knots.

"Wren told me your girlfriend has a pest problem you're helping her control. I find that not only honorable, but also admirable. I don't want you worrying about walking out on the meeting. Your mother took over fantastically. She's very passionate about this business and making sure it's advertised right. She's a gem to work with," he said.

I snickered. "Meaning, she almost chewed your ass off with some stuff."

"Yes, but on the other hand? I wish I worked with more clients that knew exactly what they wanted. It makes our jobs exponentially easie—oh! They just sent on my end. The files are big, so give it a second."

I toggled the mouse of my laptop and saw the email slide into my inbox.

"Got it," I said.

"Perfect. Want to tell me what you think?" he asked.

"Actually, it sounds like I should leave that up to my mother."

He chuckled. "We can do that too. Though, your mother tells me you run your own freelance accounting business on the side?"

"Kurt."

"I'm not going to start pitching you anything. Yet. But, expect a nice phone call from me once we get this new arena of our small businesses established. I'm going to be running a special for the first few small businesses that utilize our services."

"Uh-huh. Well, I can't honestly say I've got time in my schedule to take on new clients that advertising might bring in—"

"But, it would give you social proof. A way to build a social media outpost for your brand. Which would help you in establishing higher prices for your business going forward, if you'd like. Marketing doesn't just work to bring in clients. It works to give proof to the name behind the business. Which is just as important."

I grinned. "You're good at this."

"Eh, I get by."

I chuckled. "Thanks for taking my phone call. I'm sure both of us will hear from my mother any second on the mock-ups you've sent me. So, stay by your phone."

"It's an office day for me, so I'll be here."

"And thank you, Kurt. Again."

"No thanks needed for what you're doing. Though, I appreciate the phone call."

"Of course. We'll talk soon."

"Talk soon."

I hung up the phone call and felt better about things as I went through the motions of the day. I spoke with some of my accounting clients on the phone. I sent out weekly reports of their estates and tweaked a few things in my software on my end. Many of them wanted video conferences within the next couple of weeks. Which wasn't unfamiliar territory, seeing as the stock market had taken a substantial dip that week. But I came with reassurances. Little monikers I'd picked up over the years that always helped clients during times like these.

Playing stocks is a long game. Not a day-to-day game.

Your volatility is high because you want to produce returns. But that will come with substantial dips. The good thing now is you can buy cheap and watch the profits roll in once the market rebalances.

We just came out of one of the biggest bull markets in the past two decades. There will be some fluctuation. But nothing that will drain your assets.

Once lunch rolled around, it pulled me from my office day trance. I decided to get out of my office for lunch too. Walk across the street to the diner and get myself a nice hot bowl of, well, something. Pasta or soup. Maybe a nice hot sandwich too.

But I also wanted the space to call Sadie without people breathing down my throat.

"Well hey there, handsome."

I smiled. "You seem in high spirits."

"I am. Especially now that I have a handle on this dictation software."

"How's it coming along?"

"You know, it doesn't suck. Though, formatting is still by hand. And trying to do that left-handed is a very tedious process."

"You need anything?" I asked.

She snickered. "Just for my body to heal so I can get back to my office."

I jogged across the street. "Already feeling cooped up?"

"Not really. I just don't like the fact that some of my freedom has been ripped away from me by something I can't control. That's what I'm trying to avoid, you know? I feel like a sitting duck this way."

"Do you want me to come over after work? Not to hover. But, just to alleviate some of that *sitting duckness*."

"Then, we'd both be sitting ducks."

I grinned. "Not if I took you out for dinner."

"Oh, now there's a nice idea. Where were you thinking?"

"I don't know. I figured you might have an idea of where you'd enjoy going since you're the one cooped up at home. Speaking of which, I take it that call with your editor went okay"

She sighed. "It went as well as could be expected. On the one hand, it's frustrating not having me at work. But, on the other hand, I can work from home. So, they want me to take the next couple of weeks and work from home. Recuperate. Rest. And after I can get out of these bandages and, you know, see out of my eyeball, we can get me back in the office."

"Well, I know you were worried about that phone call. I'm glad it went okay."

"Yeah, me too."

I walked into the diner. "So, you think about what you'd like to do for dinner, and I'll make sure it happens. If there's a place you want to eat at, or if you just want to order in, or if you want me to bring something from the city—"

"Can you bring some sour cream doughnuts with you?"

I paused. "Oh no. Not you too."

"What?"

"Those things are nasty as hell."

"What?! They're amazing!"

"No, they're gross."

"You're crazy, Troy. They're the greatest doughnut to ever exist. And I'd like some, please. We don't have a Dunkin' around here."

I snickered. "I swear, my mother sinks her talons farther into you every single day."

She giggled. "Well, if I'm going to be sticking around, get used to it. Your mother's got great taste in doughnuts."

"She just loves sweet bread. If it's a carbohydrate and it's got sugar, she'll eat it."

"Ah, a woman after my own heart."

I laughed as I sat down in a booth.

"But, yes. I'll bring you some of those nasty-ass doughnuts. Any other requests?"

She hummed. "Mmm, just you in something nice to look at."

I scoffed playfully. "Wow. Just a piece of meat to gawk at, huh?"

"My good eye needs something to keep it entertained while its partner is healing. Might as well be the handsomest man I know."

My heart skipped a beat. "You're amazing, you know that?"

She giggled. "I can't wait to see you tonight."

"Neither can I. I'll be there around six. And we'll do anything you want for dinner."

"What if I want you to eat those sour cream doughnuts off my body for dinner?"

I faked a heave. "Maybe I can cover you in chocolate sauce, too, to hide the taste."

"What if I said you could spend the night with me if you eat them?"

I paused. "Do you want me to spend the night?"

There was a long pause and I waved the waitress off that wanted to approach me. I didn't want this moment to be ruined. Not if the answer was what I really, truly wanted it to be.

"It is lonely here, when Uma's not around. And—"

I sat on the edge of my seat. "What is it, Sadie?"

She sighed. "I know I've been really hard on you and my parents lately. I guess I just felt like people were hovering. Or felt as if I couldn't take care of myself. Or felt as if my life had to come to a grinding halt for some piece of shit guy who didn't deserve to control my life that way."

I nodded. "And all of that is understandable."

"But, I do miss holding you at night. I do miss waking up to you. And my mornings have been a bit rough with trying to get out of bed by myself. I stiffen up pretty badly."

"It's done," I said.

"What?"

"If you're struggling in the mornings and you need help, I'm there. No matter where you want me to sleep."

"What if I wanted you to sleep with me? Would that be too selfish to ask after how I've acted?"

I sighed. "No, Sadie. You're in an impossible situation right now. One that most people can't even fathom. I'm just glad you want me back around."

"I'm so sorry I ever made you feel as if I didn't want you around."

"I'll come with clothes to stay the night, all right? And I'll let Mom know that I'll be late coming into work in the morning. I want to make sure you're nice and loose and moving on your own before I leave you."

"Oh, sounds ... exciting."

Electricity sizzled through my bones. "I can always make it exciting."

She giggled. "I'll see you tonight, then. Don't forget the doughnuts, and plan on me trying to make some of this up to you."

"You don't have to make up anything to m—"

"Just give me the opening, Troy."

I smiled salaciously. "Okay, then. I'll come prepared for you to make this up to me."

"Good. See you around six."

"See you then, beautiful."

Chapter 23

Sadie

I reached for another doughnut as I leaned against Troy's strong chest. The Christmas movie playing on the television held most of my attention. But, not all of it. The Chinese takeout was settling. The doughnuts were fueling me with a sugar high I needed to burn off somehow. And as I felt my plan coming together, a smile crossed my face.

"What?" Troy asked.

I giggled. "Just thinking."

"About what?"

I snuggled deeper into him. "About how nice this feels."

"It does feel nice, doesn't it?"

"A Christmas movie. Wonderful food. Great company. All we need is a fire in the fireplace and we're all set."

"I could start one up, if you want me to."

I grinned. "Don't you dare move a muscle from this spot."

He chuckled. "Fine by me."

As the movie played on, I felt his hand slide down my waist. Down to the bow around my robe that kept it adhered to my body. I nuzzled against him. Underneath his chin. The doughnuts were quickly forgotten about as his hand traveled along my skin, pulling my robe up to feel the smoothness of my legs.

"Naughty, naughty," I said, giggling.

"You're the one who decided to wear nothing but this robe of yours," he murmured.

I yawned playfully. "And on that note, it's time for bed."

"Wait, what?"

I giggled as I hopped off the couch.

"I'm ready for bed. What about you?" I asked.

Troy stood up. "Are you really tired?"

I smiled. "I'm ready for bed, yes."

"Well, then allow me to escort you there."

"Troy, what ar—oh!"

He scooped me into his arms as giggles fell from my lips. I kicked my feet playfully as he smiled and carried me over to the stairs. My head fell against his shoulder. I wrapped my arm around his neck. And as he carried me into my bedroom, I felt my heart come alive.

"Lay me down," I said softly.

He eased me along the bed before reaching his foot out. He kicked the door closed, never once wavering his beautiful eyes from my own. I smiled up at him. I ran my hand along his arm. Feeling my fingertips rumbling over his muscles as he licked his lips.

"Do you want me to go?" he asked.

I wanted to answer him, but I figured what I had planned would work just as well. So, I let my hand fall to the bow around my waist and I tugged on it. I pushed the fabric back. I watched his eyes slowly dance down my body, taking in the silken black lingerie I had on underneath. The peekaboo panties had a hole in the crotch and the lacy bra barely covered my nipples. And the stockings. Oh, the thigh-high stockings made Troy practically growl as his eyes snapped back up to mine.

"Come get me, big guy," I said, grinning.

His lips fell to my neck and a soft gasp left my mouth. I arched into him, the pleasure pushing the soreness of my body away. I wanted this damn sling off my arm. I wanted the bandage around my eye to disappear. But, I wanted Troy more than anything.

And I didn't want to wait another second to feel him.

"Damn, you're sexy as hell." He growled.

"I've missed you so much." I gasped.

My good arm wrapped around his neck as he kissed down my body. As he nuzzled at my breasts. As his tongue lapped at my clothed, yet puckered, peaks. I felt his hands sliding farther down. Spreading my thighs to reveal how soaked my panties had already become. The second his fingertips fell against my bare pussy lips, he grunted. His body rushed down my own before he hit his knees, spreading me farther apart.

"Oh, you little minx." He growled.

I fisted his hair as he lapped up my slit. Flicking my clit and soaring me into the heavens. I didn't care how much I hurt. How sore I was. How far behind I was on my pain medication. I missed this. I missed him. Feeling him and kissing him and touching him.

And making love to him.

My eyes flew open. Love. Is that what I felt for Troy? The electricity that surged through my body shut down my brain. But the feeling still stuck. The buzzing of my heart. The clenching of my gut. The way my body jumped for him with every stroke of his tongue.

Could it be?

Was it possible?

Had I fallen in love with Troy?

"Oh, fuck. Yes. Yes. Yes. Holy shit." I moaned.

"Come for me, Sadie. Do it," he commanded.

"Troy!"

I arched my back as my jaw unhinged in silent pleasure. My eyes rolled back, forcing fireworks to burst behind my eyelids. I quaked for him. I felt my pussy walls succumbing to the emptiness of my body as his tongue soared me to extravagant heights. I felt alive. Wanted. Beautiful.

Loved.

My back dropped down against the bed and he kissed up my body. Leaving a trail of wetness behind him until his eyes found mine once more. I cupped his damp cheek. I gasped for breath as my body shivered beneath his. I swallowed hard, gazing into the eyes of the man who had swept me off my feet.

Time, and time again.

"Are you okay? Was that too much?" he asked.

Yes, I do love this man.

I smiled. "If anything, it wasn't enough."

He chuckled before his lips pressed against mine. And when they did, he flipped us over. I squealed as I straddled him, his legs hanging off the edge of the bed. But, I felt his raging erection underneath me. Throbbing. Pulsing. Aching, to be inside me.

I wanted him there too.

I pressed my hand against his chest and rose up. With my ass in the air and my knees against the mattress, I kissed Troy as he pulled his cock out. We didn't have any time to waste. Not a second to spare. And as the tip of his thick dick caught against my entrance, I slid down his girth. Inch by inch.

Until our hips connected.

"Oh, shit, Sadie." He groaned.

I sighed. "Troy, you fill me so good."

"I've missed you."

His hands gripped my hips as I rose up.

"I've missed you too," I whispered.

He showed me how he wanted me. He rolled my hips and made me bounce as his cock grew thick against my walls. Juices dripped down his balls. We spiraled into an endless abyss as my breasts bounced with every movement I made. His hands massaged me. Held me against him. Showed me the way to please him as I drank in everything he had to offer me. I ground against his pelvis. He bucked up into my body. His hands fisted my hips and held me still, fucking his cock with my pussy.

Until we both unraveled at the same time.

"Yeah. Sadie. Holy fuck. I'm coming. I'm coming. I'm coming."

"Troy, it's—I—you—oh, yes."

I collapsed against him and he held me close. He kissed my forehead as his dick filled me to the brim with hot, thick threads of arousal. I felt him pulsing. My pussy milked him for all he had as our bodies shook together. Quaking, in mutual pleasure, as my face fell into the crook of his neck.

"I love you. I love you. I love you so much."

The words tumbled from my lips so effortlessly. They felt so right. So appropriate. So true to how I was feeling. Troy tensed underneath me, and I wondered if I had misspoken. If I should've kept things to myself.

Until he flipped me over with his cock still sheathed in my warmth.

"Did you mean that?" he asked.

I heaved for air as sweat dripped down the sides of my face.

"Yeah. I did," I said breathlessly.

He grinned. "Good. Love you too."

Then, his lips found mine once more before he pulled himself out from between my legs.

Right before slamming himself back inside.

Chapter 24

Troy

"So, how did the finalizing of the account go with Kurt today?" Paris asked.

I swallowed my massive sandwich bite. "I finally got the paperwork signed and Mom on board with things. By the end of the month? The first three billboards will be up around the city."

She grinned. "I think this calls for a celebratory dessert. Don't you think?"

"You just want an excuse to get the biggest slice of cheesecake imaginable."

"With strawberries drizzled on top. Can't ever forget those."

I grimaced. "I don't know how you eat fruit topping like that. Fruit is made to be crunchy."

She snickered. "Yeah, say that to the fruit puddings you inhale like it's nothing."

I paused. "You mean my yogurts?"

"Same difference."

"No. Not even kind of."

She giggled. "So, what's with the lunch invite? And an offer to take a half-day? Something's crawled up your ass."

I shrugged. "I don't know. Can't I spend time with my sister?"

She narrowed her eyes playfully. "What are you feeling guilty about?"

I snickered. "The fuck are you going on about now?"

"Come on. Spit it out. What'd you do?"

"What? I didn't do shit."

"The last time you did something this nice for me, you felt like shit because you ran into the back of my car with your damn bike and busted out the light. Did you hit my car again?"

"No."

"Did you break something of mine?"

I rolled my eyes. "No. I just want to do something nice for—"

"Did you demote me? Cut my salary? Plant a pipe bomb in my plumbing at my apartment?"

I paused. "What the hell goes on in that head of yours?"

She laughed. "This will be easier if you just tell me why you've had such a guilty look on your face through this lunch."

I sighed. "It's just—with everything going on lately and with how much has changed, I just..."

Paris put her sandwich down and nodded.

"You didn't want me to think you had forgotten me," she said.

I shrugged. "In a manner of speaking."

"Troy, I promise you, it's okay. Yes, a lot has changed. But, I also know you could never forget me. I'm much too annoying for that."

I chuckled. "You said it, not me."

"And besides, I know you'd be spending more time with me if the love of your life hadn't come swooping in like she did."

I blinked. "What?"

"Oh, stop being so damn thick-headed. Everyone sees it."

"Sees what?"

"How in love you and Sadie are."

"I don't—"

"Cut the shit, Troy. It's me you're talking to. I knew you were in love with her two weeks ago when I saw the look in your eye when she walked in the door for class one day. You've got it bad, man. Just admit it."

I grinned. "I do love her, Paris."

"I knew it! Yes!"

I furrowed my brow. "I thought you just said—"

"I mean, I had an inkling. But now that I have it confirmed? Yes! This is awesome, Troy! Does she know? Have you told her? Are you going to make it romantic and shit like that?"

I snickered. "Actually, we've already told each other about our feelings, yes."

She gasped. "How did it go? How did she take it? What happened?"

"A man never fucks and tells."

She squealed. "Oh. My. Gosh! And she said it back? Full stop?"

"Full stop, Paris."

"Holy shit. Holy shit. Holy shit. I never thought you'd move on from that Holly bullshit. Oh my. Troy. I'm so fucking happy for you."

Paris got up and gave me a massive hug. One I accepted without a second thought. I felt good about things. Really good about them. In some ways, I felt unstoppable. Which was a nice feeling, considering the bullshit life had thrown at us lately.

"Paris?" I asked.

"Yeah?" she murmured.

"Can we continue eating?"

She released me quickly. "Yes, yes, yes. Sorry. I just—I'm so fucking happy for you it's sick. Seriously."

I smiled. "So, has Wren talked with you about anything lately?"

"What do you mean?"

Shit. "I don't know. About how he feels. Or about how you feel. Or anything like that?"

She paused. "What do you know?"

I held up my hands. "I know nothing."

"Troy, you tell me right now if—"

"Paris, whoa, whoa, whoa. Take a breath."

She pointed at me with her fork. "Has he told you something?"

"Depends. Has something happened?"

She narrowed her eyes. "Are you the one who gave him the idea of Niagara Falls?"

"So, he asked you."

"You knew?!"

I chuckled. "Come on, Paris. Cut the man some slack. He was wanting to make sure he made the right move. You know, not doing a weekend getaway too soon or some shit like that."

She sighed. "Well, I love the idea. He surprised me with the tickets a few days ago and we've been trying to plan a weekend ever since. I'm really looking forward to it, if we can settle on something that works for both of us."

"Something going wrong with the planning?"

But, when she looked over at me, I knew what she meant.

"Sadie isn't going to take offense to the two of you wanting to get away for a weekend," I said.

"I know, I know. I just don't want to leave her when things are like this, you know?" she asked.

"Well, she's got me, and Uma, and Mom. You know damn good and well Mom will pack her guns up and stay in Sadie's house whether anyone wants her to or not. You know, if she feels it's right," I said.

"You think?"

I took Paris's hand. "I know. Plan the weekend with Wren. In fact, take the rest of the day and do it now. Pick a weekend, book a hotel, and make plans with the man. Don't put your life on hold for this shit. We've got it covered."

She smiled. "You're the best."

After we finished lunch and I covered the tab, Paris rushed out the door. Probably to go bug Wren on her half-day to get plans solidified. However, there was still one more important woman in my life I wanted to talk with. A woman I wanted to make sure wasn't suffering or feeling neglected ever since Sadie had come into my life.

So, I started back for the gym and headed to my mother's office.

"Knock, knock," I said.

I opened the door and found Mom hunched over her desk. Scrawling her chicken scratch across some paperwork.

"I don't have long, sweetheart. What's up?" she asked.

"Well, I'll get to the point, then," I said.

"Something on your mind?"

"I wanted to come by and make sure you didn't feel as if I had forgotten about you with all this time I've been spending with Sadie."

Her pen stopped moving and she slowly looked up at me. Her brow furrowed tightly together before she stood from her chair. And I watched her face slowly morph from confusion into that cheeky smile of hers.

"You worried your poor mom can't take some competition?" she asked playfully.

"It's not a competition," I said.

"Oh, I know that, you crazy person. This bad boy exterior you always sport has made me laugh more times than I care to count. Deep down, I know you've got more love to give in this world than the best of us. And plus, you're a momma's boy. You'd never be able to neglect me if you wanted."

I snickered. "I suppose that's true."

"Come here and give me a hug, sweet boy."

I walked into my mother's office and she wrapped me up tight. Even though I was two times her size, her arms always felt as if they encompassed the whole of me. I closed my eyes. I breathed her in. I relished the warmth of her being as we stood there in her office. She rubbed my back softly. Like she always did whenever she hugged me close.

Then, she pressed a kiss to my cheek.

"I like this one. So, don't fuck it up," she whispered.

I chuckled. "I'll try not to, Mom."

"Good boy."

I stood up from the hug. "Oh, by the way, I gave Paris a half-day."

"Yeah, I figured you would."

"What?"

She giggled. "You've been walking around this place looking guilty as fuck for days now. I'm surprised it took you this long to ante up like you always do with her. You're so predictable, you know."

I blinked. "This is insane."

She laughed. "I wouldn't have you any other way, though, sweetheart. But, if she's taking a half-day, then I think you could use one too. It's our slowest day. I've got things here."

"No, no. I've got too much work to—"

She cupped my cheeks. "Go home, Troy. Give yourself some time to breathe. It's been a hell of a past few weeks. Give yourself some time to rest."

"Okay. I can do that."

"Good. And clean that nasty-ass apartment. I know you haven't been keeping up with it with how much time you've been spending over at Sadie's lately."

I grinned. "I guess you do know me well."

"Seriously. Clean that place up before it becomes a nuclear hazard zone with the city."

"It's not that bad, Mom."

"With boys? It's always that bad."

And with one last kiss to my cheek, she dismissed me from her office.

After shutting down my computer and locking up my office, I made my way home. The walk was cold, making me shiver down to my bones. I shoved my hands into my pockets. I burrowed as far down into my scarf and my jackets as I could. The wind hurt my eyes. Made them water as I walked toward my condo complex. But, the second I walked down into the garage, a wild hair worked its way up my ass.

Might as well start with cleaning my bike.

I grinned as I walked past my beautiful motorcycle winking at me from its parking spot. I hadn't properly cleaned her down in a couple of months now. Really, ever since Sadie had come into the picture. My bike needed some tender loving care. And I needed a little while longer to work up the courage to start cleaning my place.

But, when the hairs on the back of my neck stood on end, I froze.

"Hello?" I called out.

I slowly turned around to see who the hell was behind me.

"Anyone there?" I asked.

All I heard was the echo of my voice off the corners of the garage, though.

You're getting paranoid, Troy.

Something was off, though. Something wasn't right. And as I shoved my hand into my pocket to find my cell phone, I turned my attention to the little screen. I wanted to call Sadie and make sure she was okay. I wanted to hear her voice and reassure myself she was fine. That I was being hypervigilant. That I was psyching myself out.

But that didn't stop me from quickly hustling toward the elevator the second the doors slid open.

Chapter 25

Sadie

"Detroit Metro Times, this is Sad—"

"Sadie, you need to get to the gym now," Paris said.

I furrowed my brow. "Why, what's going—?"

"Troy's gone."

"What?"

"Troy's missing, Sadie!"

I blinked. "Slow down. Take a breath. What's going on? Fill me in."

"I tried calling Troy this morning when he didn't show up for work. His mom went by his place. I called Wren, had him try calling Troy. No answer. He's not answering anything."

"And he's not at his place?"

I heard typing on the other end of the phone as I stood from my seat at the kitchen table.

"Paris!" I exclaimed.

"Sorry, sorry. That was Katie. No, Troy's not at his place. And according to her, both his car and his bike are in the garage. You need to get over to the gym. Are you at work?"

"No, I'm working from home for another couple of days. All my work calls are being routed through my—"

"Can you drive? I mean, if you really needed to?"

I shook my head. "I don't know. I don't—how long has Troy been off the radar?"

"I wanted you to know what was going on, but Wren's got a few other places he's looking. Troy apparently took a half-day like me yesterday, so there are a few other places he could've gone to get some rest or something."

"Well, he's not here. I haven't seen nor heard from him."

"I'll call you the second I know something. Okay? In the meantime, Wren's on standby to come get you, just in case?"

I blinked. "Just in case what?"

She sighed. "Hopefully, nothing. I'll call you soon. Okay?"

Tears rushed my eyes as Paris hung up on me. I flopped back down into my chair and hugged my knees to my chest. Troy. He was gone? Where had he gone to? And without his bike? Or his car?

None of this smelled right.

"Shit." I hissed.

I opened up a text and sent one to Uma. I knew she was in the middle of her shift and wouldn't be able to pick up her phone. But she had thirty minutes to message me back. And if she didn't? I'd be calling the hospital myself to check on her.

Me: Don't ask. Just let me know you're safe at work.

Then, I set my phone down and waited.

I didn't have to wait long, though. Because a few minutes later, it started ringing.

"Uma? Are you all right?" I asked.

"*Uma*? What's wrong with Uma?" Wren asked.

I sighed. "Nothing. Just checking up on her. What's going on? What have you found?"

"It's not good, Sadie. I came to pick up Troy's mom from his place and decided to poke around. There are signs of a struggle near the elevator. There's blood on the corner of it."

I felt my face pale. "Bl-blood?"

"I've got guys coming out here now, but I want you to call the police on your end too. Luke's back."

Tears rushed my eyes. "Are you sure it's him? I ... I ... I mean, it could be anyone's blood. Right?"

"I think you know, in your heart of hearts, that's not the case."

I sniffled. "Oh no."

"Paris is headed for your place now to come sit with you. Don't go anywhere. Do you hear me?"

I drew in a broken breath. "Yeah, I hear you."

"Good. As I get updates, I'll call you. But I'm serious. Call the police on your end and alert them. Tell them to contact me directly for any information they might need."

"Okay," I whispered.

"Paris will be there soon. Just hang tight."

Then, I got hung up. Again. Before a text rolled through my phone.

Uma: I'm fine, girl. What's up?

I felt sick to my stomach. I stood on wobbling legs as I tried texting her back what was going on. But it was no use. My fingers were shaking too much. I couldn't keep control of my faculties. And as tears flooded my neck, it grew harder to breathe.

"Troy. No. Not Troy."

I bent over as my heart fluttered in my chest. I gripped the edge of the kitchen table and closed my eyes. I swallowed hard before spitting on the floor. Because it felt as if my entire throat had closed itself off.

Deep breaths through the nose, Sadie. Come on. You can do it.

But, I didn't feel like I could do anything right now.

The heavy knock on the door scared me. So, I rushed into the kitchen. The massive knock continued, like a fist against my door, as I unsheathed a knife from the wooden block on the counter. I slowly walked toward the door. The pounding of it in my ears made my heart stop in my chest as I slowly reached for the doorknob.

"Who is it?" I asked.

"Let me in. It's me," Paris said.

"Oh, thank fuck." I breathed.

I ripped the door open and let the knife fall to the floor. Paris barreled through the doorway, wrapping me up tightly in her arms. And as she kissed my cheek and my head, I broke down.

"Not Troy. Please. Please tell me it's not him," I said through my sobs.

"It's okay. If it is him, we'll find him. All right?" Paris asked softly.

But, I knew the truth. I knew what had happened. And none of us knew where he was. Or what Luke had done with him. Or if he was still even alive.

"It's okay. I've got you," Paris whispered.

And as we made our way over to the couch in my living room, I collapsed in a fit of sobs.

Feeling more helpless and more useless than I'd ever had in my entire fucking life.

Chapter 26

Troy

"**H**ey! What the fuck is wrong with you?!"

The second I came to, I started yelling. The smell of the moldy van made me sick to my stomach. But, the taste of blood in my mouth made me furious. I tried moving my arms and legs. But to no avail. There was something tight cinching against my skin. Something akin to plastic, digging into my joints.

Zip ties.

"Hey, you cowardice fuck! Let me out of here!" I bellowed.

Because I knew exactly who had done this to me.

My head pounded with the worst headache alive. No, no. Migraine. It made me sick to my stomach and jiggled my vision with every pulse behind my eyes.

"Hey!" I roared.

I scooted around as much as I could. Trying to find anything to rake the zip ties against. A wrench, or a loose piece of metal. Or even a sharp-ass corner. But there was nothing. Every time I moved, my head felt like it split further down the middle. Even my fucking self-defense moves didn't release me from the bonds around my wrists and ankles.

What the fuck?

"Luke!" I roared.

I felt helpless. Lying there, on the floorboard in the back of some fucking van. Was Sadie all right? Had something happened to Paris? Or my mother? Where the hell had this asshole brought me?

Was he about to try and kill me?

Footsteps falling against the floor caught my ear. My blood boiled with readiness. I wanted nothing more than to strangle that little fucker until his eyes popped out. And as the back doors of the van fell open, my suspicions were confirmed.

"Well, I guess you aren't the big meathead idiot I thought you were," Luke said.

I snarled. "Why don't you unleash me and we can see who the fucking idiot is."

"I suppose letting you loose would make me a major idiot. So, I think I'll pass."

I lunged at the man, but all he did was laugh. Laugh. He fucking laughed in my damn face. To see that coward's face made my vision drip red. Never in my life had I understood the need to kill. The need to take someone's life. But as I lay there—staring at that fucker's little grin—I understood. Every crime show, every psychopath, every confusing need.

I understood why people killed and enjoyed it.

"Look at this big man. All tied up. Helpless, while I stand here. I know you think you're better than me, with your tattoos and your muscles. But, you're an accountant, Troy. I mean, who the hell sleeps with an accountant?"

I rolled my eyes so hard I was surprised they didn't fall out.

"You have me at your mercy and those are your last words?" I asked.

He chuckled. "Hardly last words."

"You're an idiot. She left you. Deal with it, asshole."

Luke lunged at me in the back of the van. "She may have left me. But she doesn't have you anymore, does she? And once she realizes you're not coming back, she'll be mine again. I'll swoop in, patch up that broken heart of hers, and she'll look at me again like she used to. With pride. With love. With respect."

I chuckled. "Or you could—I don't know—try not hitting her. That might work."

Luke bellowed out a psychotic shriek before I felt something hard come down against my jawline. I groaned as his knuckles connected with my face, and I wondered why it hurt as bad as it did. Shit. He probably did a number on me while I was unconscious. Either that, or I'd really rolled around in the back of the van while he dragged me off to fuck-only-knows where.

"Shit." I hissed.

"I know how to love Sadie better than you ever will. And once you're out of the picture, she'll come to her senses. She'll see that. I know she will." He glowered.

I spit blood onto the floor. "Yeah. Let me know how that works out for you."

His fist came down against my face again and blood pooled against my tongue. I didn't grunt, though. I didn't make a sound. I didn't give him the fucking satisfaction of it. No matter what Luke thought—and no matter how bad things felt right now—I knew this guy wasn't going to win. He couldn't. There's no way in hell an idiot like him outsmarted a man like me.

And he sure as hell wasn't putting his hands on Sadie again.

Not as long as I was alive.

"You go ahead and make yourself comfortable back here. Because you'll be here for a while," Luke said.

"What? Don't have the balls to kill me?" I asked.

I heard him jump out of the van. "Nothing to do with having balls."

"Oh, yeah? Then, what does it have to do with?"

I twisted my aching neck over toward him just in time to see a psychopathic smile stretch across his cheeks. A smile that shivered even me to my core.

"It has to do with figuring out just how I want to kill you," he said.

And as his chuckles filled the space around me, he slammed the van doors closed.

Chapter 27

Sadie

"Wren, you know how this goes. You can't put a missing person's report out—"

"For fuck's sake, who gives a shit about the rules?! Troy's missing, Kiner! Come on!" Wren exclaimed.

"And until twenty-four hours have passed, we can't put out a report unless you got an eyewitness to his kidnapping."

"This is bullshit and you know it. You know damn good and well the blood we found at the crime scene is his." He hissed.

"And when we get the lab back proving that, we'll take steps. But damn it, Wren, you gotta stand down for a bit and let us do our jobs."

I put my head in my hands. As Uma and Paris rubbed my back, I listened to Wren argue with the cops down at his station. Sitting at the house did me no good. I felt like people were watching me from all angles. So, I had Paris drive us all down to the station so we could be closer. Just in case Troy showed up.

"This is all my fault," I whispered.

"It's not your fault. This is all Luke," Paris said.

"Yeah, Sadie. You had nothing to do with this," Uma said.

"I got him involved in the first place when we started seeing each other. We never should've started anything. I never should've asked for his help in the first place," I said.

"And you know damn good and well that would've never flown with him," Paris said.

"I need someone to listen to me. Get Clausey on the phone. He's the one heading up this Luke case," Wren said.

The arguing over at the police's desk grew as the three of us sat there. Worried, trying not to cry, and thinking the worst had already happened.

"Wren, I'm not calling that man tonight. It's his wife's birthday," the other officer said.

"Kiner, if I have to call that man myself, I'll be personally letting him know what kind of a shitbag you are. Now, if you don't wanna listen to us, then get that man on the phone. Now," Wren said.

"You aren't going to threaten me like that. Cop or not, there's protocol. You don't get to usurp that protocol just because a friend of yours is in trouble."

"And you don't get to call the shots just because you're on the clock and parked behind that fucking desk. Now, get Clausey on the phone, or I'm calling the chief on his fucking vacation over this!" he roared.

"Wren." Paris hissed.

He whipped around and glared at us before pulling out his cell phone. I leaned against Uma and sighed heavily as the two men continued to argue at the desk. I didn't want them to argue or fight any longer. I just wanted someone to find Troy.

"Chief. Yeah, hi. It's Wren. Sorry to bother you on your *vacation*—"

"Are you fucking kidding me?" The other officer glowered.

"—but, we have a bit of a—wait, you know?" Wren asked.

I shot up from my seat and made my way for him.

"What's going on?" I whispered.

Wren held his hand out. "Uh-huh. Yeah. No one's talking to me about anything. Yes, I know I'm personally involved now. Yeah, but—Chief—yes—no one is telling me anything. That's the issue. If there's something to tell, as family of the victi—no, I'm not blood relat—"

I yanked the phone from Wren's hand. "Hello?"

"Who's this?" the gruff voice asked.

"Hi there. Sir, I'm sorry. My name is Sadie Powers. My boyfriend is the one who's been supposedly taken by my ex," I said.

"I'm sorry for what's going on right now," he said.

"Me too. And I'm sorry it's taken you away from your vacation. I don't want anyone to break any rules. But, the only shred of Troy's family right now is trying the best she can to hold down an entire business because he's missing. And we can't relay information to her we don't have. I don't know what's going on and I don't know how protocol works, but I'm begging you, please. Tell me what's going on," I said.

I felt Wren staring at me. Hell, the whole of the station seemed to be staring at me. And all I hoped was that my plea worked.

"Get into a private room and put me on speaker," Chief said.

"Thank you, thank you so much," I said.

"What is it?" Wren asked.

"We need a private room. Now," I said.

I glared at the front desk officer before Wren took the phone back. He shuffled us into what looked like an interrogation room before closing the door behind us all. The click of the speakerphone sounded just before Paris flipped on some lights. Then, as we all huddled up, the chief's voice filled the space around us.

"All right, you guys here?" he asked.

"We're here, sir," Wren said.

"Look, there's a rush on the blood sample you found at the scene. But, the lab is always bogged down. You know this," he said.

"What else is there?" Wren asked.

"The camera footage in the garage didn't reveal much. Most of the place was dark. We've got footage of a man we believe is your friend, Troy. But, we don't have the face of his attacker."

"But, you know it's Troy, right?" I asked.

"From the enhanced pictures we're obtaining and the pictures Wren has of the man, yes. But, he's not in the system or anything, so that's all we have to go on."

"What about a getaway vehicle? Or anything like that?"

"Once Troy's pulled into the darkness, he's gone. We hear what we think is a van, and we've got someone trying to identify the tread marks left behind. But, once Troy's knocked out—"

"He was knocked out?" I asked softly.

I slowly looked up at Wren and drew in a shuddering breath.

"He surprised Troy," I whispered.

"In the video, there's what looks like a pipe. It comes down hard, then Troy hits the floor. He's dragged off, we hear the squealing of tires, and that's it," Chief said.

"Oh, no." I whimpered.

"We're going to find him, Sadie. Have faith," Wren said.

Wren and his chief talked back and forth for a little while, but I couldn't hear them. Everything passed in such a blur. The phone call ended. Then, somehow I ended up in the car. Pieces of the world flashed by as we made our way back to the house. My house. A house so far away from Troy. Someone sat me on the couch. Put a hot mug of coffee in my hand. And I hated that there was nothing I could do.

So, I fell asleep.

I didn't sleep well, of course. I tossed and turned. I got up and walked around. I went to climb into Uma's bed, until I saw Paris already there. I sighed at the sight of them. Not wanting to leave me alone, but wanting to give me space.

"I love you guys," I whispered.

I paced the house until the sun came up. I sat on the couch and let my head fall back for a nap. I woke up to the smell of coffee filling my nostrils, and I almost reached out for Troy.

Until I remembered the reality of my situation.

"Want it black, or bogged down with sugar?" Uma asked.

I sighed. "I don't care."

"You hungry?" Paris asked.

"No," I said softly.

I hoisted myself up from the couch and shuffled around the house. I needed something to do. Anything to pass the time. I had work. I could get some stuff edited. I didn't have any new articles to turn in, though. And I didn't have any new places to go visit for reviews. I ran my good hand through my hair. I hated feeling so helpless.

Fresh air. I need fresh air.

"I'm going to get the mail!" I exclaimed.

"Wait a second, someone needs to go with you," Paris called out.

But, I was already out the door by the time she finished her statement.

The cold winter air slapped me across the face. I shivered from head to toe. My entire body locked up with the chilly subfreezing morning, and it made me feel alive. I felt. It hurt, but I felt. And as I drew in the cold air through my nostrils, I opened my mailbox.

Only to find a folded-up piece of paper with my name on it.

"What the—?"

"Sadie! You need a damn coat!" Uma exclaimed.

I reached into the mailbox and picked it up as Paris rushed out to me.

"Put this on, you insane human being." She breathed.

And as I unraveled the note, I felt my world come to a grinding halt.

TAKE ME BACK, AND HE DOESN'T DIE.

THE END

Tenacity

TENACITY

LEANING TOWARDS TROUBLE SERIES

USA TODAY BESTSELLING AUTHOR

LEXY TIMMS

Leaning Towards Trouble Series

Book 1 – Trouble
Book 2 – Discord
Book 3 - Tenacity

Find Lexy Timms:

LEXY TIMMS NEWSLETTER:
http://eepurl.com/9i0vD
Lexy Timms Facebook Page:
https://www.facebook.com/SavingForever
Lexy Timms Website:
http://www.lexytimms.com

Want

FREE READS?

Sign up for Lexy Timms' newsletter
And she'll send you updates on new releases,
ARC copies of books and a whole lotta fun!

Sign up for news and updates!
http://eepurl.com/9i0vD

More by Lexy Timms:

FROM BEST SELLING AUTHOR, Lexy Timms, comes a billionaire romance that'll make you swoon and fall in love all over again.

Jamie Connors has given up on men. Despite being smart, pretty, and just slightly overweight, she's a magnet for the kind of guys that don't stay around.

Her sister's wedding is at the foreground of the family's attention. Jamie would be fine with it if her sister wasn't pressuring her to lose weight so she'll fit in the maid of honor dress, her mother would get off her case and her ex-boyfriend wasn't about to become her brother-in-law.

Determined to step out on her own, she accepts a PA position from billionaire Alex Reid. The job includes an apartment on his property and gets her out of living in her parent's basement.

Jamie must balance her life and somehow figure out how to manage her billionaire boss, without falling in love with him.

** The Boss is book 1 in the Managing the Bosses series. All your questions won't be answered in the first book. It may end on a cliff hanger.

For mature audiences only. There are adult situations, but this is a love story, NOT erotica.

Faking It Description:

HE GROANED. THIS WAS torture. Being trapped in a room with a beautiful woman was just about every man's fantasy, but he had to remember that this was just pretend.

Allyson Smith has crushed on her boss for years, but never dared to make a move. When she finds herself without a date to her brother's upcoming wedding, Allyson tells her family one innocent white lie: that she's been dating her boss. Unfortunately, her boss discovers her lie, and insists on posing as her boyfriend to escort her to the wedding.

Playboy billionaire Dane Prescott always has a new heiress on his arm, but he can't get his assistant Allyson out of his head. He's fought his attraction to her, until he gets caught up in her scheme of a fake relationship.

One passionate weekend with the boss has Allyson Smith questioning everything she believes in. Falling for a wealthy playboy like Dane is against the rules, but if she's just faking it what's the harm?

Book One is FREE!

SOMETIMES THE HEART needs a different kind of saving... find out if Charity Thompson will find a way of saving forever in this hospital setting Best-Selling Romance by Lexy Timms

Charity Thompson wants to save the world, one hospital at a time. Instead of finishing med school to become a doctor, she chooses a different path and raises money for hospitals – new wings, equipment, whatever they need. Except there is one hospital she would be happy to never set foot in again—her fathers. So of course, he hires her to create a gala for his sixty-fifth birthday. Charity can't say no. Now she is working in the one place she doesn't want to be. Except she's attracted to Dr. Elijah Bennet, the handsome playboy chief.

Will she ever prove to her father that's she's more than a med school dropout? Or will her attraction to Elijah keep her from repairing the one thing she desperately wants to fix?

THE ONE YOU CAN'T FORGET

Emily Rose Dougherty is a good Catholic girl from mythical Walkerville, CT. She had somehow managed to get herself into a heap trouble with the law, all because an ex-boyfriend has decided to make things difficult.

Luke "Spade" Wade owns a Motorcycle repair shop and is the Road Captain for Hades' Spawn MC. He's shocked when he reads in the paper that his old high school flame has been arrested. She's always been the one he couldn't forget.

Will destiny let them find each other again? Or what happens in the past, best left for the history books?

** This is book 1 of the Hades' Spawn MC Series. All your questions may not be answered in the first book.

Did you love *Discord*? Then you should read *Just Me*[1] by Lexy Timms!

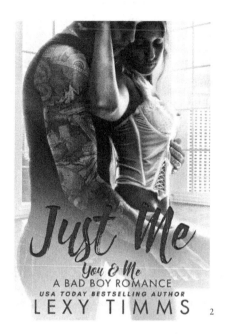

We all need somewhere where we feel safe...

After leaving her abusive husband, Katherine Marshall is out on her own for the first time. She's hopped from city to city to avoid the man who made her life a living hell. When it seems she's finally found a new place where she begins to feel safe, she slowly grows confident that her life is looking up. A chance meeting with Ben O'Leary sets her life on a course and her soul on fire.

Ben launched a business that went on to viral success while he was in college, and now as a thriving entrepreneur, he's most interested in maximizing profits. A billionaire living the dream But all that changes when he sets his eyes on Katherine. Things between the two heat up

---

1. https://books2read.com/u/bP58Q7

2. https://books2read.com/u/bP58Q7

as they fall hard and fast—that is, until she gets an unexpected surprise that will test the strength of their relationship.

You & Me - A Bad Boy Romance

Book 1 – Just Me

Book 2 – Touch Me

Book 3 – Kiss Me

Read more at www.lexytimms.com.

Also by Lexy Timms

A Bad Boy Bullied Romance
I Hate You
I Hate You A Little Bit
I Hate You A Little Bit More

A Burning Love Series
Spark of Passion
Flame of Desire
Blaze of Ecstasy

A Chance at Forever Series
Forever Perfect
Forever Desired
Forever Together

A Dating App Series
I've Been Matched
You've Been Matched

We've Been Matched

A "Kind of" Billionaire
Taking a Risk
Safety in Numbers
Pretend You're Mine

BBW Romance Series
Capturing Her Beauty
Pursuing Her Dreams
Tracing Her Curves

Beating the Biker Series
Making Her His
Making the Break
Making of Them

Billionaire Banker Series
Banking on Him
Price of Passion
Investing in Love
Knowing Your Worth
Treasured Forever
Banking on Christmas

Building Billions - Part 1
Building Billions - Part 2
Building Billions - Part 3

Change of Heart Series
The Heart Needs
The Heart Wants
The Heart Knows

Conquering Warrior Series
Ruthless

Counting the Billions
Counting the Days
Counting On You
Counting the Kisses

Diamond in the Rough Anthology
Billionaire Rock
Billionaire Rock - part 2

Dirty Little Taboo Series
Flirting Touch
Denying Pleasure

Dominating PA Series
Her Personal Assistant - Part 1
Her Personal Assistant Box Set

Fake Billionaire Series
Faking It
Temporary CEO
Caught in the Act
Never Tell A Lie
Fake Christmas
Fake Billionaire Box Set #1-3

Firehouse Romance Series
Caught in Flames
Burning With Desire
Craving the Heat
Firehouse Romance Complete Collection

Forging Billions Series
Dirty Money

For His Pleasure
Elizabeth
Georgia

Madison

Fortune Riders MC Series
Billionaire Biker
Billionaire Ransom
Billionaire Misery

Fragile Series
Fragile Touch
Fragile Kiss
Fragile Love

Great Temptation Series
The Devil's Footsteps
Heaven's Command
Mortal's Surrender

Hades' Spawn Motorcycle Club
One You Can't Forget
One That Got Away
One That Came Back
One You Never Leave
One Christmas Night
Hades' Spawn MC Complete Series

Hard Rocked Series
Rhyme
Harmony
Lyrics

Heart of Stone Series
The Protector
The Guardian
The Warrior

Heart of the Battle Series
Celtic Viking
Celtic Rune
Celtic Mann
Heart of the Battle Series Box Set

Heistdom Series
Master Thief
Goldmine
Diamond Heist
Smile For Me
Your Move
Green With Envy

Highlander Wolf Series
Pack Run
Pack Land
Pack Rules

How To Love A Spy
The Secret
The Secret Life
The Secret Wife

Just About Series
About Love
About Truth
About Forever

Justice Series
Seeking Justice
Finding Justice
Chasing Justice
Pursuing Justice
Justice - Complete Series

Kissed by Billions
Kissed by Passion

Kissed by Desire
Kissed by Love

Leaning Towards Trouble
Trouble
Discord
Tenacity

Love You Series
Love Life
Need Love
My Love

Managing the Billionaire
Never Enough
Worth the Cost
Secret Admirers
Chasing Affection
Pressing Romance
Timeless Memories

Managing the Bosses Series
The Boss
The Boss Too
Who's the Boss Now
Love the Boss

I Do the Boss
Wife to the Boss
Employed by the Boss
Brother to the Boss
Senior Advisor to the Boss
Forever the Boss
Christmas With the Boss
Billionaire in Control
Billionaire Makes Millions
Billionaire at Work
Precious Little Thing
Priceless Love
Gift for the Boss - Novella 3.5
Managing the Bosses Box Set #1-3

Model Mayhem Series
Shameless
Modesty
Imperfection

Moment in Time
Highlander's Bride
Victorian Bride
Modern Day Bride
A Royal Bride
Forever the Bride

My Best Friend's Sister

Hometown Calling
A Perfect Moment
Thrown in Together

Neverending Dream Series
Neverending Dream - Part 1
Neverending Dream - Part 2
Neverending Dream - Part 3
Neverending Dream - Part 4
Neverending Dream - Part 5

Outside the Octagon
Submit
Fight
Knockout

Protecting Diana Series
Her Bodyguard
Her Defender
Her Champion
Her Protector
Her Forever

Protecting Layla Series
His Mission
His Objective

His Devotion

Racing Hearts Series

Rush

Pace

Fast

Regency Romance Series

The Duchess Scandal - Part 1

The Duchess Scandal - Part 2

Reverse Harem Series

Primals

Archaic

Unitary

RIP Series

Track the Ripper

Hunt the Ripper

Pursue the Ripper

R&S Rich and Single Series

Alex Reid

Parker

Saving Forever

Saving Forever - Part 1
Saving Forever - Part 2
Saving Forever - Part 3
Saving Forever - Part 4
Saving Forever - Part 5
Saving Forever - Part 6
Saving Forever Part 7
Saving Forever - Part 8
Saving Forever Boxset Books #1-3

Shifting Desires Series

Jungle Heat
Jungle Fever
Jungle Blaze

Sin Series

Payment for Sin
Atonement Within
Declaration of Love

Southern Romance Series

Little Love Affair
Siege of the Heart
Freedom Forever
Soldier's Fortune

Whisky Harmony

The Bad Boy Alpha Club
Battle Lines - Part 1
Battle Lines

The Brush Of Love Series
Every Night
Every Day
Every Time
Every Way
Every Touch

The Debt
The Debt: Part 1 - Damn Horse
The Debt: Complete Collection

The Fire Inside Series
Dare Me
Defy Me
Burn Me

The Golden Mail
Hot Off the Press

Extra! Extra!
Read All About It
Stop the Press
Breaking News
This Just In

The Lucky Billionaire Series
Lucky Break
Streak of Luck
Lucky in Love

The Sound of Breaking Hearts Series
Disruption
Destroy
Devoted

The University of Gatica Series
The Recruiting Trip
Faster
Higher
Stronger
Dominate
No Rush
University of Gatica - The Complete Series

T.N.T. Series

Troubled Nate Thomas - Part 1
Troubled Nate Thomas - Part 2
Troubled Nate Thomas - Part 3

Undercover Series
Perfect For Me
Perfect For You
Perfect For Us

Unknown Identity Series
Unknown
Unpublished
Unexposed
Unsure
Unwritten
Unknown Identity Box Set: Books #1-3

Unlucky Series
Unlucky in Love
UnWanted
UnLoved Forever

War Torn Letters Series
My Sweetheart
My Darling
My Beloved

Wet & Wild Series
Stormy Love
Savage Love
Secure Love

Worth It Series
Worth Billions
Worth Every Cent
Worth More Than Money

You & Me - A Bad Boy Romance
Just Me
Touch Me
Kiss Me

Standalone
Wash
Loving Charity
Summer Lovin'
Love & College
Billionaire Heart
First Love
Frisky and Fun Romance Box Collection
Beating Hades' Bikers

Watch for more at www.lexytimms.com.

About the Author

"Love should be something that lasts forever, not is lost forever." Visit USA TODAY BESTSELLING AUTHOR, LEXY TIMMS https://www.facebook.com/SavingForever *Please feel free to connect with me and share your comments. I love connecting with my readers.* Sign up for news and updates and freebies - I like spoiling my readers! http://eepurl.com/9i0vD website: www.lexytimms.com Dealing in Antique Jewelry and hanging out with her awesome hubby and three kids, Lexy Timms loves writing in her free time. MANAGING THE BOSSES is a bestselling 10-part series dipping into the lives of Alex Reid and Jamie Connors. Can a secretary really fall for her billionaire boss?

Read more at www.lexytimms.com.

Made in the USA
Monee, IL
26 April 2022

95458770R00148